Dutch Jo and her Good Time Girls

Sara Van Donge

Dedicated to Josephine Wolfe and the real working ladies of Walla Walla.

Dutch Jo and her Good Time Girls

Sara Van Donge

Chapter One

Dutch Jo in San Francisco

Josephine was beautiful at twelve. In fact, she would be beautiful her whole life. The blonde, cool beauty so admired by the men in San Francisco had arrived with her parents the previous winter, though she hadn't had much time to enjoy her new country before both had fallen ill and died. Young Jo had been forced out of their small boarding house when her work as a seamstress had failed to make the rent and, after two nights sleeping on the edge of a filthy tent city in the oppressive fog, she had followed a cheerful girl named Liza to The Saint Louis Hotel. Jo and Liza were a beautiful pair of sunshine, and the bartender at the hotel easily welcomed them into his establishment as they peeked through the heavy door.

"Well, hello there Miss. Liza, it seems you've found a friend." He greeted them as Liza led Josephine into the parlor. The Saint Louis Hotel was comfortably laid out with velvet sofas and damask settees arranged so visitors could have private conversations. The long wooden bar was well-stocked and the bartender was dressed smartly in a crisp white shirt and black vest. Though Jo was very nervous, she felt more comfortable now that she saw the beauty of her surroundings. The room was empty, though it held the energy of a place that was generally full of people.

Liza greeted the bartender with a casual wave. "Jo needs work too, my kind of work. Is Madge up yet?" Liza had confidence, Jo had to give her that. And what she lacked in education she made up for with her bright smile and quick wit. Her English was perfect, where Jo's native German made her a figure of scorn if she did not carefully choose her words.

The bartender shook his head and called out behind him, "Madge, Liza came back, we told you she wouldn't be gone long!"

A giant woman appeared, wiping her hands on a dirty apron covering a too-fancy dress. She squinted appraisingly at Jo.

"So, you're back, hmmm?" She asked Liza, but her eyes were on Jo, taking in her slim good looks.

Liza drew herself up and smiled, her bright blue eyes sparkling.

"Yes, but Madge - I will not join the ladies until I am fourteen. And neither will Jo."

Madge laughed. "Is that right? And how do you plan to earn your keep?"

Liza held up her chin and looked the older woman right in the eye, speaking with a confidence that impressed Jo. "Madge, you know you want this to be a highly regarded establishment. You want your gentlemen to visit The Saint Louis because the ladies are experienced and sophisticated. Not frightened, crying little girls."

Madge nodded smartly, "You are absolutely correct young one. I have often said the same. We have plenty of ladies already and we certainly do need some help with the cleaning and cooking. Now go find your friend an apron and help Hortencia."

And with that Jo began working at one of the middle-level bordellos in the San Francisco Red Light district.

True to her word, Madge did not pressure either girl to begin working until the age of fourteen. But Jo and Liza were watching and learning. By the time the appointed age arrived, they were eager for their opportunity to earn much more than they had cleaning after all the revelers had left.

Chapter Two

Liza

Liza began her life in a parlor house in New York City, her mother was a prominent lady of the night known as English Rose, though her friends called her Rosie. By the time Liza was able to talk she called her Rosie too.

Rosie had arrived in New York from England with her mother after her father died in a shipping accident. Both young Rosie and her mother soon found themselves living in a filthy boarding house where her mother soon contracted pneumonia and died. Alone and destitute, it did not take Rosie long to begin working. She joined the throngs of other young girls who made money in the one of the only ways possible while living in squalor as a recent immigrant. When she found herself with young baby Liza her main concern was how to keep Liza from infringing on her busy working life. Most evenings of the week, Rosie visited different theaters around the city, her favorites were the Bowery Theater where she could enjoy being boisterous and humorous. Though she was not an actress and had never graced the stage, she was still well-known on the Third Tiers and in the Galleries for her lively wit and lovely face. She attended with her friends where they would meet gentlemen, enjoy performances, dine at different restaurants around town, and make a fine profit at the same time.

English Rose was known even at the formal and genteel Broadway Theater for her great beauty and charm. Her red hair and snapping blue eyes attracted the attention of the most financially successful gentlemen. It was here she met Mr. George Crawford, a handsome and wealthy banker. Mr. Crawford was a widower with a young daughter, Edith, who was only one year younger than Liza.

Though their backgrounds could not have been more different, Edith had attended the best private schools to study art, dance, and classical piano while Liza had hidden in the kitchen of ever-changing parlor houses, the two girls were happy to have each other and became fast friends.

Liza was only nine when her mother married Mr. Crawford and she could not believe her good fortune. Where before she would be woken by hollering girls in whatever crowded boarding house her mother had decided to live in that month, now she had her own sunny room and soft bed in the Crawford house. Before, Rosie would drag Liza with her to the Third Tier of the Bowery Theater where Liza would make herself very small hiding behind a curtain watching Rosie and other working girls laugh and coquette their way through the raucous crowd of gentlemen.

Rosie often left Liza behind with one of the cooks or maids or even alone as she went out for the evening wearing her fancy silk dresses, her cheeks shining pink, her hair glinting like copper beneath the latest style of hat. But on occasion, Rosie would bundle Liza up hastily to leave their current living situation, hurrying out the door with all their meager belongings as one landlord after another chased after them with a shaking fist.

Liza learned not to ask questions. For although Rosie had a quick laugh and ready smile, she was also prone to throwing herself into a rage if something didn't go her way. Liza knew how to stay on the good side of her young mother.

Not everyone was so lucky. Rosie often had friends who would join her in her evening activities. Liza would watch them getting ready to leave, styling their long hair, giggling, laughing and telling stories about their escapades the evening before. Rosie was scathing in her assessment of the Olympic Theater which she considered beneath her, full of bizarre acts and crude ladies. One of her many friends was Clara who had been known to frequent the Olympic. Liza knew Rosie was feeling threatened by Clara; at this point Rosie had met Mr. Crawford and felt covetous of his affections. Clara, however, had recently started visiting the Broadway theater and Rosie was on high alert.

True to form for Rosie, she kept Clara very close as a friend and confidant, with the poor ignorant Clara very much in the dark as to the true nature of Rosie's interest.

But one evening as the two were preparing to step out Clara mentioned how much she enjoyed the Broadway.

"I just love Fifth Avenue, it is so elegant and dignified." She was gushing as she brushed her black hair. "I especially love all the wealthy gentlemen, they are so much more generous than those fun-loving boys at the Olympic or even the Chatham!"

Rosie kept her smile fixed across her face, but Liza, seeing a glint forming in her mother's eye, slipped out the door into the hallway. This seemed like a good time to visit with one of the maids.

Within moments she could hear her mother screaming, accusing the poor unsuspecting Clara of spending too much time talking to Mr. Crawford, telling Clara she was unattractive and irritating, hissing how no one enjoyed her company.

Rosie was at the end of the hall as Clara flung open the door, her hair still down and flying around her face.

"You belong on Water Street!" Rosie screamed after her, as she fled down the stairs. "No, Canal! Canal is where you should go! You belong in a low-class dance hall!"

Of course they never saw Clara again, nor did Rosie even mention her. Liza watched her turn back into her room, a small triumphant smile playing on her pretty lips, pleased to have eliminated a rival.

But now things were different. Rosie stored away her flashy silk dresses and jeweled hats, replacing them with equally elegant but more subdued dresses made of the finest linen, wool, and silk. Now, she spent her days organizing her large and elegant household, planning with the head cook, directing the maids, and seeing to it that both Edith and Liza received the best private schooling.

Liza was shocked in the change in her mother and still kept a wary eye on her at all times, but the comfort and security provided by Mr. Crawford, with his big mustache and cheery stories, seemed to give Liza a new view on life. Within a year the family had settled into a routine and Liza was beginning to grow, both physically and emotionally.

Her haphazard early years had left Liza thin and nervous, her yellow hair and pale skin had often sparked inquiries into her health. Never knowing from one morning to the next where she would eat or sleep had left her anxious and quiet. But now, after a year, she was plump and healthy. Her hair had a golden shine and her blue eyes had begun to sparkle. Most importantly, she had lost her shifty-eyed, hunch-shouldered stance and was now calm and relaxed.

It was Rosie becoming a mother that led to this dramatic shift, yes, but more than that it was Edith, her new sister, who had directed Liza to a new life.

Edith was gentle and good-natured, like her father, but unlike her father she had an innate understanding of the inner workings of people. Though she loved her new mother and had never bore witness to her screaming wrath, she seemed to understand the difficulty Liza had gone through. She offered her new sister a steady friendship that gave Liza the strength to grow.

Though Edith herself had suffered the loss of her mother, she did not feel grief from the incident as it had happened when she was born. Mr. Crawford had loved his dear first wife, and had many sweet stories to tell Edith about her mama, so, although she had slipped away just two days after Edith was born, Edith still felt her mama had been a positive presence in her life.

The two young girls led a charmed life in New York, visiting Central Park with Rosie and Mr. Crawford or their tutor, dancing and singing at the School of Arts, enjoying literature and handicrafts in the comfort of their large home. Then, Mr. Crawford came home from the bank one evening anxious about a great-aunt who had fallen ill in London.

"Her manservant contacted me via todays post," he was telling Rosie at dinner, "I haven't seen Great-Aunt Edna since I was a boy, I hope they are looking after her. She was always such a dear."

Liza and Edith payed little mind to the conversation of the adults, the Crawfords had very few relatives save one elderly aunt who lived in New Jersey and had not approved of Mr. Crawford's marriage to Rosie. Aunt Agnes had not attended the wedding and had never visited their house. This new Great-Aunt was of little consequence to two young girls, they were much more caught up in their own world of dollhouses and pretend.

Edith and Liza passed any free moment playing with Edith's beautiful dollhouse, a replica of their own house complete with furnishings and dishes. They had created a world of their own and while Edith sewed clothing for the dolls, Liza enjoyed creating stories and intrigues for them. It occupied their imaginations, and it was while kneeling in front of the dollhouse one week later that they heard Mr. Crawford burst into the house and call to Rosie in alarm.

The two girls looked at each other in confusion, it was mid-morning and Mr. Crawford was always at the bank at this time. What was he doing home? They crept out to the landing to listen.

"She passed away in the night, I need to go to London to settle her affairs. I shall not be gone more than fortnight." Mr. Crawford was saying to Rosie.

"Can't you postpone it? The weather has been so harsh lately. Can't you wait until spring?" Rosie asked her husband.

But he couldn't, and within days he had packed and gone and the house was a little less cheerful in the evenings. Within two weeks, however, the house became much less cheerful when a telegram arrived informing Rosie that her husband had not arrived; his ship had encountered a storm and sunk. All aboard were lost.

And as abruptly as their good fortune had come it was taken away. After one short year, Liza was wrenched from her newly found life of comfort, security and, most importantly, Edith.

Of course Rosie had tried to remain in their home, she had pleaded with Mr. Crawford's aunt Agnes who had swooped in immediately to claim not just Edith but the house and all it's contents.

"How dare a woman of your class attempt to ingratiate your way into my brothers home and wealth!" Aunt Agnes had sneered as she stood watching Rosie pack, ensuring she took only her possessions. "I know who you are!"

Rosie's fury had not come as quickly as it used to, and for once when her anger erupted Liza felt triumph instead of fear.

Her blue eyes flashing, Rosie's voice rose to cover the nasally whine of her sister-in-law.

"How dare you turn me out of my home! How dare you take Edith from us! You are an unkind witch of a woman and I would wish you nothing but ill-will if it weren't for that treasure of a child hiding from you in her room! You do not know what you are doing, you are destroying not just my life but hers as well!"

With a flounce, she had pushed past Agnes and called out to Liza, who had huddled with Edith; both girls terrified of the sudden changes they couldn't control.

Liza had turned and watched her sister and best friend as she left, both with identical expressions of grief and loss, as Agnes slammed the door behind them. Liza sobbed as if her heart would break.

Rosie, showing a strength Liza had never realized her mother possessed, marched immediately to a jeweler and sold all the jewels her husband had given her, including her diamond wedding ring. In this way, Rosie was able to buy a ticket for herself and her daughter to Independence, Missouri, and then on to San Francisco.

"There is gold in California." She explained to Liza as they prepared to join a group on one of the first wagon trains out that spring.

The journey, though difficult, was cathartic. Walking slowly along behind the wagons and animals, Liza was able to let her mind rest and heal from the pain. She tried not to think about how Edith must be suffering, having to live with Aunt Agnes, she consoled herself knowing Edith at least had material comforts, something that was in short supply on the trail west.

Chapter Three

Golden Streets of San Francisco

Arriving in San Francisco was like stepping into a new world. Where New York was bustling and crowded like their new home, San Francisco was filled with a frantic materialism unlike anything Liza had ever seen. The Gold Rush was in full swing and the wealth moving through the city was like an electric current. The scarcity of women made any female the subject of arduous attention and within days Rosie had thrown herself back into her profession. Though this time she was being paid in gold, and plentifully.

Rosie's priorities had never been particularly motherly, though in their year of comfort living with Mr. Crawford and Edith she had shown Liza more care and consideration. Now that she was again spending her evenings working, she had once again begun to focus her attention on her own appearance, the purchase of beautiful dresses and sparkling combs and jewels.

At first they established residence in a tent city known as Chilitown on Telegraph hill. Rosie had been apprehensive of the many Latina girls living in small, hastily constructed shacks and tents, but once they were living and working side by side, their differences were unimportant when compared with their similarities. Liza quickly made friends with the other children who ran freely through the narrow walkways, enjoying the freedom and camaraderie they shared.

San Francisco was growing quickly, new miners and treasure hunters arrived daily both from the harbors and the trails. Rosie and the other ladies were able to bring in more money than they had ever imagined. Before the first cool winds of winter had a chance to blow in, a group of girls, led by an older red-head named Madge combined what they had together and rented out a newly built parlor house near the American Theater.

When Liza moved into her new, more permanent residence she was thrilled to have an address so when she wrote to Edith she could give her a way to respond.

Up until this point, Liza had been mailing letters but without a return address she had no hope of a response. Now she could hear how her step-sister was faring with her aunt.

Dear Edith

Rosie and I are here in San Francisco, it is one wild place. Are you fine? Is that mean aunt treating you nice? Does she ever let you out of her sight? We finally found a regular place to live, at first we went to this awful tent city called Chilitown, it was just terrible. You would not have survived. It is lucky I was poor for so long because we had to sleep on the ground just barely covered with blankets. Rosie was scared it would rain and we would never get dry. There are so many people everywhere, but I miss you and papa and our comfortable house and our dollhouse and our books and all of it. It is crazy here, so much gold and people. At least there are other little girls, we live in a hotel they called The Saint Louis and Honoria and Ana are good to me. I miss you.

I don't see Rosie as much as I want, she works every night and worries again, like she did before you and papa came. She drinks whiskey and I hate it, it makes her laugh hard and say mean things. She gets headaches too, but the doctor gave her laudanum so she feels better. She misses you too and sends her love.

Please send us a response. I have included the address. We miss you and love you.

Love always

Liza

Liza knew it could be many months before she received a reply, but she continued to write, taking comfort in the familiarity of a conversation with Edith, even if it was only one sided.

Though the parlor house, which the ladies had decided to call 'The Saint Louis' after Madge's home town was more comfortable than the temporary tent they had first occupied, the gentlemen who poured into the parlor and dining room were coarse and loud. Liza and two of her friends, Honoria and Ana, watched through a narrow slit in the doorway to the kitchen as their mothers entertained their high-paying guests. Honoria and Ana had both been born in Mexico, though they too had recently arrived in San Francisco with their mothers. When Liza pressed them for information they both lowered their eyes and mumbled about the Mexican-American war. Liza knew from the pain in their faces not to press for more information.

Ana, who at twelve was just beginning to blossom into a young woman, spoke a halting English that Liza found charming. Her round, dark face and black eyes were serious and she was the responsible older sister who made sure all the younger children were looked after and, most importantly, quiet and kept out of the way.

On this evening the smaller children were all in their shared room, sleeping, and Ana was telling Honoria and Liza that her mother expected her to begin working too.

"She say I pay own way, now, I cost too much." Ana whispered as they sat on the floor peeking out into the crowded dining room.

Juanita, who was Ana's grandmother, was wiping up the counters, preparing for the onslaught of dishes she and the girls would clear from the dining room.

"Ay, m'hija." She said in her soft voice, brushing the hair back from Ana's worried face. "No te preocupes amor mia. Aguantate." Honoria whispered to Liza that Juanita was telling her it would be OK, she could endure it. Not to worry.

Ana replied, tears streaking her round cheeks, and Liza did not have to speak Spanish to understand that her friend had no desire to join her mother in the boisterous activities in the next room. Liza was eleven now and could feel the men looking at her when she and the others scurried out with Juanita to clear the tables. Though the ladies guided them into the parlor after they ate, some men seemed more interested in lingering behind to watch her and the other young girls. It made Liza feel ill. She knew her yellow curls attracted attention, but until this year she had never felt the burning gaze of a man and it filled her with a dread that began in her chest and dripped down her stomach.

Rosie had not said anything about it, but Liza knew it was only a matter of time. Ana was still speaking softly to her grandmother, who stroked her hair and cooed soothingly to her in Spanish. Juanita's cheeks were also streaked with tears, though she hid her face from her granddaughter, wiping them brusquely away.

"Ya, ya." She finally said, sounding angry, though her round, wrinkled face showed it was actually grief and despair. "Ya eres grande, secate las lagrimas y ya." She shooed the three girls out into the dining area where the gentlemen were following their mothers and the other ladies to the parlor.

Madge, an older woman who collected payment and ensured order between the gentlemen and the younger girls, passed them as they came out. Seeing Ana's tear-streaked face she hustled them right back into the kitchen.

"What is this?" She asked Ana, looking into her face.

"My mama, she - she want me work too. I start tomorrow." Ana said softly, looking at the floor.

Madge looked at Juanita who continued with dishwashing, pretending to not hear the exchange.

"This is not right. No gentleman wants to see a teary face and a reluctant girl. What are these ladies thinking? We never would have done it this way back home" She muttered, her face growing red enough to match her fiery hair. "I will talk to your mother tomorrow Ana, she needs to understand that this is not good for you - and it is not good for business."

Giving Ana a quick hug, she turned and marched back out to the Parlor. But Ana's mother did not want advice from Madge.

The next morning Liza, Ana, and Honoria watched from their hiding place behind the drapes as Madge spoke to Hortencia. Hortencia set her lips and shook her head, insisting that she had three other small children to feed as well as her mother. Ana would work too.

As Honoria and Liza stayed behind to help Juanita, Ana joined the other ladies as they prepared to entertain their gentlemen for the evening. Rosie had seemed unconcerned when Liza mentioned the unfolding drama.

"Ana is overly sensitive!" Rosie had declared flippantly, not even looking up at her daughter from the elaborate beaded dress she was mending. "She won't mind too much, we all do what we need to and the pay is our bread and butter."

Here she looked up at her daughter, as if seeing her in a new light. "And I do see Hortencia's dilemma, Ana will bring in enough income they won't have to worry, they will all live more comfortably. Everyone needs to contribute, your day will come soon enough."

Liza had wanted to respond, but she could not think of an argument that her mother would not carelessly ignore. Going back to her own mending, Liza began to form a plan.

"Honoria," she said that evening to her friend as they washed the dishes. "Has your mother approached you yet about beginning work?"

Honoria didn't even hesitate, "Oh yes, I will start when I am twelve, like Ana. I still have over a year but my days back here, cleaning and cooking, are numbered." She seemed so unconcerned that Liza began to wonder if maybe their fate was not so bad after all.

Honoria spoke Spanish and came from Mexico, like Ana and her family, but she was very different looking. Her light brown skin had a golden glow that Liza envied, so different from her own milky white skin. Honoria was bold and outspoken and her easy laughter was infectious.

"My mom and her sister have been preparing me for a long time," she was saying as she dried a platter, "they have given me some instruction and explained what I can do. I know it isn't fun, though on occasion it might be better than always cleaning and cooking and caring for all the babies."

Liza considered this possibility. Her mother certainly seemed to enjoy herself, though her headaches were getting worse and she was spending more and more of her days lying in bed. But at night when she emerged and went into the parlor, her loud laughter could be heard throughout the house.

"And do not forget how much fun it will be to wear beautiful clothing!" Honoria declared, her eyes finally settling into a smile as she contemplated her fate. Though Honoria was trying to be cheerful, her eyes gave her away. Liza could sense she was not being entirely truthful but was instead trying to convince herself.

The next morning, Honoria and Liza lingered near Ana's door, presumably cleaning, waiting for her. When she finally emerged they shyly approached, asking how she was. She was surprisingly calm though she had little to say. She only looked at the floor and shook her head, holding her arms around herself. Her mother came up the hallway and found them standing near her door.

"What is this? What you tell my daughter?" She asked Honoria and Liza, then she spoke with vehemence to Honoria in Spanish. Liza tried to follow along with the small amount of Spanish she had acquired, but the most she could ascertain was that Hortencia was angry at both Hororia and Liza for interfering. She said the word metiche at least three times, gesturing threatening toward both girls. Liza wanted to shrink back from the angry woman, but she did not allow herself to be weak. Instead, she breathed deeply and clenched her jaw. Ana may not be able to stand up for herself, but no one could stop Liza from helping her friend.

"This is not right!" She said defiantly, her blue eyes blazing. "You know Ana is too young, we all are. If a gentleman wants a young girl like us, then maybe he should go to a less dignified place."

Hortencia stopped mid-speech and stared, gaping at Liza. Then she recovered her wits and, pulling Ana toward her, she guided her daughter back into her bedroom. Calling over her shoulder before she slammed the door she yelled, "You leave us alone or I see to it you mom get you working too."

Left alone in the hall, both Honoria and Liza were stunned at the hatred they had seen on Hortencia's face. They felt as though they had been wronged, they had only been trying to offer their friend support and kindness, not infringe on her working life. But now Ana's mother saw them as enemies.

After that they rarely saw Ana, she stayed in her room most days, only emerging with her mother to scurry down the stairs after her mother to join the other ladies in parlor for work in the evening. After a few months, it was as if they had never been friends at all.

By the time Liza was twelve, her thin body had filled out and men had started to notice her. One evening, as she worked with Honoria in the recently vacated dining room, a spindly little man named Mr. DePier lingered behind the rest of the guests. He stood in the doorway, watching the two girls as they cleared the dishes from the table. Liza could feel his eyes burning into her and it gave her a sick feeling in her stomach.

When she entered the kitchen with Honoria she turned to her friend in horror, "What is he doing?" Liza whispered.

"He has always disgusted me, I see him here every Friday night." Honoria replied.

"I know! That little mustache and the way he always fondles his mouth." Liza said, shuddering.

When they returned to the dining room for the table cloth and napkins, Mr. DePier was still there, leaning comfortably against the doorframe, stroking his lips and staring at Liza. He exuded a smug confidence that made her angry.

"Yes?" Liza asked, her voice clear and steady. "Can we help you?"

"I'm sure you most certainly can Miss. Liza." He said, his voice overly low, as if he had practiced. He kept his eyes steadily on hers and she understood his meaning clearly.

"I am not available to help anyone. I am a child." Liza said, shaking inside but breathing slowly to steady her voice.

"I would not say that, look in the mirror. I think you and I could work out a good trade, I already spoke to your mother and she thinks it is an excellent idea."

Liza's breath caught in her throat, was this true? It was certainly possible, twelve was not too young in many estimates and she knew her mother had been considering her upcoming birthday. But not with Mr. DePier! Backing out of the room, she bumped into Honoria who had been standing just behind her.

"I am not prepared, Mr. DePier. Please find some other girl." She stammered, her confidence evaporating under his predatory stare.

Honoria finally managed to squeak out, "Liza is too young. She needs time." As they both scurried back toward the kitchen.

Once safely out of Mr. DePier's penetrating gaze, both girls looked at each other in horror. They had known the time would come, it was inevitable. Ana now was comfortable with her situation, though on occasion she now took the time to speak to Honoria or Liza, stealing away to share the latest gossip. She confided that the work wasn't really that bad, once you got used to it. Madge kept the lowest men out and tried to keep the drinking and carousing to a minimum. But Liza was not ready, she needed time.

Marching up the back stairs, she slipped into the room she shared with Hortencia and three younger children. Careful not to make noise that would wake the sleeping children, Liza quickly packed her meager belongings into a bundle and pulled on her thin cloak. Hortencia had followed her and watched in horror as she realized what Liza was about to do.

"Where will you go? If you think Mr. DePier is bad, remember the gentlemen that would come see our mothers on Telegraph Hill!" Hortencia whispered furiously as they emerged into the long hallway.

Shrugging her off, Liza scurried back down the stairs, giving her friend only the briefest of glances before waving goodbye.

Once on the dark street, Liza's conviction started to fade. Where would she go? It wasn't as if she could just go knock on the door of a pretty house and ask for shelter, nor could she return to Edith at her Crawford home. After walking for many blocks she found herself in Chilitown, the tent city where she and her mother had first taken refuge. The many hastily constructed shacks were often draped with blankets and gunny sacks, reminding Liza of the forts she and Edith had made on occasion, row upon row of makeshift shelters. Finding a tree surrounded by shacks and blankets on all sides, Liza took comfort in the cover of darkness as she curled up and attempted to sleep.

The ground was hard and her thin cloak did little to protect her from the chill of the fog, but Liza did manage to get a little sleep. She awoke with a start, however, when she heard yelling near her.

"Get out! What are you doing? This is my space you little rat!" She heard the fierce shrieking of a woman's voice cutting through the pre-dawn air.

Sitting up quickly, Liza scanned her surroundings, making sure the anger was not being directed at her. What she saw not ten feet from her was a girl no bigger than herself backing away from a small tent, her hands out. Though Liza knew it was impossible, the girl looked like Edith. Could it be? Had Edith received her letter and followed her out here?

"Forgive me, I thought it was vacant." The girl said, the trace of an accent in her voice revealing she was not Edith.

"Vacant! A lady can't go to work and have her home taken over by some miscreant?" The older woman was still yelling. Liza had seen enough drinking to recognize that she had clearly had too much.

Without thinking Liza jumped up and strode over to the girl who appeared frozen in terror. Grabbing her arm, Liza said with confidence, "There you are! Let's go!" and pulled her away from the still yelling woman.

The girl who shared Edith's delicate features and fair coloring clutched Liza as they hurried away. "Thank you," she said gratefully, "I didn't know what to do. I thought she might hit me."

Liza directed her toward an outcropping of trees overlooking the tents where they could sit. As the sun rose over the hill the two girls shared stories. Jo had only that day left the small boarding house she had shared with her parents. They had died of consumption leaving her with no relatives in the city. She was scared but her strength was evident, she remained calm as she described her tragedy.

Liza had stopped thinking of her as Edith, though the resemblance made her feel a connection to the new girl. As the sun was warming the fog away she confided in Jo about her lost step-sister and her fear in joining her mother in her profession.

Josephine looked intently at Liza as the older girl explained what her mother did, she wrinkled her nose at the description of the loud gentlemen and the smarmy Mr. DePier, but when Liza told her the ladies had made enough working to be able to open The Saint Louis she perked up.

"You mean, the gentlemen pay every time?" She had asked, "and Madge collects it?"

Liza nodded, "Well of course, haven't you ever talked with a working girl before?"

Jo shook her head, her eyes wide. "No, we are Catholic, my parents would cross the street if we even had to walk by one of their establishments. But..." She looked Liza up and down, appraisingly, nodding her head, "you are obviously well-cared for and you say you grew up this way?"

Liza was slightly uncomfortable, she giggled and pushed her new friend back, "Stop staring! I'm not a horse for sale! Yes, I am well-cared for! Though my mother and the other ladies have their flaws, our house is a good place to be."

Jo hesitated, looking shyly up at Liza. "Do you think they would take me in? I'm quiet, I don't take up much space?"

Liza suddenly realized that dealing with the likes of Mr. DePier, while safely protected by other ladies, was preferable to the indignity of sleeping on the ground and starving. And besides, she hadn't actually spoken to her mother or Madge, maybe they would see her way of thinking if she explained why she was not yet ready to begin working.

Standing up, she nodded at Jo. "Yes, come with me, I'll take you to The Saint Louis!"

Francisco Caldaron was the only child of a Mexican banker and an elegant singer, though he had been raised by his grandmother, Abuelita Conchita, after his mother died. Though the Calderon Family was from Texas, they had always considered themselves Mexicans. It wasn't until the Treaty of Guadalupe Hidalgo in 1848 that Franciso discovered he was suddenly an American citizen. His family had always lived in Texas, though Franciso and his grandmother often traveled to Mexico to visit his father and other relatives. When he was 25, he married a delightful young lady named Elena and it looked like he would settle into a life of family and raising cattle. But Elena had died in childbirth, just as Franciso's own mother had a quarter of a century earlier, and when his Abuelita died just a few weeks later of sudden congestive heart failure he realized he had to make a sudden change to his life.

Francisco had traveled further from the hills of San Diego toward San Franciso to seek a better life. And for awhile he had it. His Abuelita Conchita had taught him to play the piano when he was a boy. Though she had never been wealthy, his grandmother had worked as a governess for a wealthy Spanish family in Mexico City when she was a girl, learning the piano as well as dance, embroidery and French alongside the children. When the war had broken out the wealthy Spaniards had returned to their homeland, leaving Conchita with her love of music, to find a new life for herself. Though she had never made much use of her knowledge of French, dance, or embroidery, she did teach her only grandson to play the piano. A skill he found very useful years later when he found himself alone in San Francisco during the Gold Rush.

Franciso met Madge at a dance. He wandered in one evening, just two days after arriving in town. He was wearing his favorite cowboy hat, a deep brown felt with a red band and genuine horse-hair lanyard, but he realized his Texas ways weren't quite the look everyone else was sporting in this newly wealthy city. As he sat awkwardly looking out over the packed dance floor, he contemplated returning to his boarding house. He was looking for work, and hoped to get an early start the next morning, but the lively music had called to him so he had stopped by. Just as he was about to stand up to go, a large smiling lady stood in front of him and held out her hand.

He jumped up, his grandmother's training had left him skilled in chivalry.

"Well, hello there, cowboy!" The lady said confidently, "It looks like you might have lost your herd somewhere around Wyoming."

The twinkle in her eye put Francisco at ease, though he still felt foolish for wearing his large hat inside this elegant establishment.

"I – I just arrived here from Texas. Francisco. Francis in English." He managed to stammer out, hoping his accented English wasn't going to scare her off. The two days he had been here had already taken their toll, he was really beginning to feel lonely, questioning why he had come this far from his family in Mexico.

"Texas! Well how do you do?" She smiled even more broadly and extended her hand, giving his a big shake before sitting in the chair next to his.

He returned to his seat and joined her in conversation, he learned her name was Madge, she ran a small but elegant hotel nearby, and she loved to visit this place to "see about the competition".

It was just about this moment when the music stopped. The piano player was shaking his left hand in pain, shaking his head sadly. His bandmates looked at him in concern.

"Oh no, not again," Madge sighed, "this has been happening to this poor player too much! He just needs to rest his hand and let it heal, stop trying to push himself. But without him - they can't perform."

Francisco looked toward the stage, looked at the piano player shaking his head, looked at the disappointed crowd...and bolted toward the stage.

"I will return in a moment!" He called back toward Madge.

And before he could change his mind or think it through, Francis Calderon was on his way in San Francisco. The crowd loved him, but Madge hired him to work at her hotel, seeing his value to her establishment, and the rest is history.

Chapter Four

Drudgery

Life for Josephine and Liza took on a comfortable rhythm at The Saint Louis. Both rose early to work with Juanita in the kitchen, preparing breakfast. Later, they took care of the cleaning, shopping, and washing. Though the drudgery left their hands chapped and calloused, they earned just a small portion of what the other ladies in the house were earning.

Honoria had followed her plan and had started joining the other ladies in the parlor to entertain gentlemen each evening. Unlike Ana, who still remained mute when asked directly about her experiences, Hortencia was outspoken and unashamed.

"Oh, the first time was awful!" Hortencia told wide-eyed Liza and Jo. "I bled! My mom told me I would, she even prepared me with some dark cloths. But the boy was not experienced and I think I might have scarred him for life!"

Her cheery account of her work made both girls feel better about the looming business laying before them. As Hortencia described the different gentlemen and their preferences, giving everyone comical names such as El Lloron for a man who whimpered or Mr. Hair for a large furry man, even Ana began to relax a little. The four younger girls would meet together regularly in the kitchen to eat breakfast before the other ladies came down, many groaning about too much whiskey or laudanum the night before.

Hortencia gave her friends another reason to see their profession as more than just a burden - the pay. Hortencia gleefully described the new dress the seamstress up the block was making for her, silk brocade with lace at the neck and three petticoats. And a matching pink bonnet with silk rosettes. Ana had little left after taking care of her grandmother and siblings, but she too, was having a red dress sewn and was eagerly awaiting her final fitting.

Josephine and Liza looked down at their drab cotton dresses, weighing the payment with the work. Eventually, after a long day of washing linens and undergarments, hanging them on the roof to dry, shining the silver, preparing, serving, and cleaning three meals, Liza decided laying down with a man for thirty minutes couldn't be that bad. As long as it wasn't Mr. DePier.

She marched up to her mother's room, prettily decorated with a pink rose coverlet and matching chaise lounge, and flopped herself down on the chaise.

"I'm ready, mama." She said dramatically.

Rosie looked at her in amusement, "You finally got tired of being a household servant, hmmm?" She asked, smiling, though her eyes showed the sadness that still lingered over her difficult life.

"Will it be terrible? Will it hurt? Is it so awful?" Liza asked.

Rosie sighed, shaking her head. "It all depends, honey. It depends on the man, more than anything. Some smell so awful and are brutish, those are the ones you just have to close your eyes and endure." She stared vacantly ahead, "Whiskey and laudanum help pass the time with men like that." She added sadly.

Liza felt panic rise up in her throat, "No! Mother, no! That sounds like the worst hell. Just laying there, all vacant, while some stinky man..." She recoiled at the idea.

Rosie, realizing she had not helped her daughter with this description, turned from her mirror and patted Liza'a back.

"No, no, my love. It isn't all bad. It can actually be a lot of fun, I promise you. A lot of the gentlemen are just that, gentlemen, and they smell fine and are polite and some even care how you feel. I know! We'll make sure you get Mr. Tony, he likes for a lady to feel special. He'll be a good one to start off with. Or maybe one of the young boys? Maybe someone to discover what you are doing on your own?"

She seemed to be going through the gentlemen in her head, contemplating which would be the best for her daughter. She held up her finger, "I know! Mr. Alexander! He's barely a boy, not much older than you, and so eager it won't take but a moment. And exuberant, silly like a dog, you'll see. All you have to do is smile and lift your skirt and he's thrilled."

It hadn't taken long for everyone to start calling Josephine Dutch Jo because of her accent, but when she protested they were careful to only call her that when she wasn't around. Up until this point both Liza and Jo had risen early while the ladies slept. They cleaned and cooked and ensured The Saint Louis was beautiful and ready to welcome patrons for the evening. They didn't work alone, Juanita carried the major brunt of the work and the younger children helped too. Plus Madge joined them later in the morning, though only to oversee.

But this afternoon, it was only Jo helping Juanita prepare the meat and vegetable stew the ladies would eat along with corn bread for their afternoon meal. Jo knew Liza had finally decided she was through with working day and night with cleaning and washing and cooking, and Jo was starting to feel the same way. They had been training a couple of the younger girls to help out more and more, and Jo was beginning to feel less apprehensive about the nature of the activities she would have to engage in upstairs.

As she chopped a pungent onion, she glanced down at her budding chest, wondering just how long it would be before she really started looking like a woman. Unlike Liza, who even at twelve had the curves and confidence of a much older woman, Jo was still small and thin. Jo's own mother had been beautiful, tall, cooly blonde, and elegant, despite having to working hard her whole life. Back in the old country she and Jo's father had struggled to keep their small farm amidst political turmoil and had been forced to leave to seek better options in this new country. For awhile it had appeared they might even be successful, they had saved and booked passage on the boat from New York to San Francisco, planning on joining the throngs of successful gold hunters. Neither had accounted for the consumption outbreak, however, and had succumbed to the illness before they had even had a chance to plan what to do with 11-year-old Jo.

But here she was, and she had gotten pretty lucky, though the pennies she was earning a day would never get her very far. When she saw the large payouts Madge gave to each lady at the end of every week after she had gone through her books, Jo knew where the money was: the gentlemen who walked through that door every evening.

Yes, Jo knew the ladies had to eventually go into one of the boudoirs alone with the men and she absolutely dreaded it...but how bad could it be? The other ladies were all nearby and no one ever complained about anything more than smell or inconsideration. Certainly Madge and Francis wouldn't let anything truly bad happen to her, right?

"How was it!" Jo asked Liza the next morning when her friend finally emerged from her room looking grumpy and disheveled.

Liza made a face, "I need coffee and breakfast."

"Was it awful Liza?" Jo's heart sank. If this was all she had to look forward to, what could she do with her life? What else was there for a young orphan girl in a town full of men? She wasn't eager to work in the mines and the cooking and cleaning were fine but the pay was barely enough to save even five dollars a week.

"No, I got Mr. Alexander. He was fine." Liza shuffled into the narrow kitchen and poured a cup of Juanita's syrupy coffee from the percolator into a teacup. Jo waited anxiously for her friend to wake up and tell her about her evening.

"Mr. Alexander, you know the one? The tall gangly one we could always hear singing along with Francis on the piano?" Liza continued, "He was nice, though I don't think he knew what he was doing any more than I did. Mama was right, he was like a puppy bouncing all over the room. He paid Madge, I'm sure, she would never let someone go for free. But he only took a couple of minutes. I don't think it's really supposed to be like that!"

Both girls laughed, the idea that a man wouldn't know what to do was a relief, maybe the life they had in front of them wasn't so bad after all.

Liza went on to describe the gowns the older ladies had worn, though Jo had seen them as they had gone down. Both girls loved the beautiful silks and brocades and the rustles of slips and could discuss fine clothing at length. Jo was more interested in what Liza and the others had to do both in the parlor and, to a much greater extent, in the boudoir. The older ladies were kind and friendly to the girls but couldn't be bothered with explaining the intricacies of their lives to girls they saw as mere children. Not to mention, all were so engrossed in the elegance and excitement and gossip of their lives they just didn't have time.

"Well, Sam came into the room with me and took his hat off." Liza explained, giggling nervously. "Then he sat down next to me on the bed and kissed me."

Juanita bustled through the tiny kitchen at this moment.

"You ladies going to work today or just waste it with chatter, chatter, chatter?" She chirped in her accented English as she zipped by with an apron full of potatoes.

Juanita had been a working girl when she was younger. Unlike other prostitutes who end up moving on to lower and lower stations, worse and worse bordellos, maybe even ending up in a mining camp or on the street, Madge and the others had encourage Juanita to join her daughter and grandchildren in exchange for caring for the apartments, meals, and the bulk of the cleaning. Of course, the ladies all were responsible for their own room cleaning, but since they could not easily leave the hotel they depended on Madge and Juanita for food and other sundries.

"I tell you what to do with them men!" Juanita said as she began chopping the potatoes into perfectly even squares, "Just do what they want long enough to get their thing out of their pants. After that all you got to do is make 'em finish up as quickly as possible and you don't gotta worry about them no more. Roll 'em over, let em sleep, and make yourself scarce. That's how you earn your keep without getting into trouble."

Liza and Jo were nodding, wide-eyed and silent. They had so many questions about this, but didn't even know where to start.

"Oh, and don't forget to tell 'em how much you liked it, how big it is, how much better he is than any other man. That always speeds the process along." Juanita chuckled, "And remember that a lot of men are just lonely. There aren't many women out here, so just be that sweet girl he needs you to be."

"And don't forget the Pessairre!" Interjected Sally cheerfully as she swept in. Sally was cute and older than many of the other ladies and often laughed and shared stories with Jo and Liza. But the Pessairre was something they hadn't heard before.

"Pessaire?" Liza asked, passing her a cup of Juanita's coffee.

"Madge didn't tell you?" Sally's brown eyes widened in alarm. "That Sam didn't do anything inside of you last night, right?"

Liza frowned, "You mean like you talked about where they groan and collapse and the sticky mess? No, I felt bad for him, I think it happened before he could get his pants off."

All four laughed at the plight of poor young Singing Sam Alexander.

"Well," continued Sally, "you have to put the Pessaire inside, the druggist delivers them here. Madge calls it the Pisser, or you can just call it the Female Preventative. It's from France. But make sure you put it inside before you come down to see the fellows. So your body thinks there's a baby. That way his seed can't go in there and make one. Why do you think none of us have babies?"

"That and Bishop's Purse." Juanita pointed to the pots of pink flowers in the windowsill, delicate purse-shaped flowers dangling at the end of tall stems.

Liza and Jo were grateful for the information but now had even more to talk about. Liza went back to the room to get ready for the day, while Jo settled into the kitchen, ready for a long day of cooking and cleaning - and maybe some more information from Juanita!

Chapter Five

Josephine's Turn

Josephine didn't have to wait long to learn first-hand what it was men wanted. Just a few short months later, Imogen, one of the older ladies, left with her favorite customer to get married. Josephine found herself getting dressed with Liza and the rest one afternoon, preparing her hair in an elaborate style as she listened to their easy chatter. Though no one else indicated the least bit of trepidation, Jo could hardly concentrate on their light conversation because of her nerves. What if she ended up injured or sick? No one seemed the least bit anxious, but Jo couldn't help but feel panic rise up in her throat.

She tried to relax and calm herself as they descended the elegant staircase into the main parlor later that evening. There were a handful of gentlemen scattered about, some holding serious conversations around smoking cigars, others reading newspapers. Francis played a lively tune on the piano and Sally immediately started swaying the full skirt of her dress in a cheerful little dance. Her big smile and easy laugh attracted the attention of an austere gentleman with a full mustache and an expensive-looking suit. He rose and approached her, extending his arm. Sally ducked her head giving him a coy smile as she reached up and took his arm. Jo could hear Sally murmuring and giggling softly as she led the gentleman back up the stairs toward the boudoir.

Well, that seemed easy enough. Thought Jo, slightly annoyed with her own shy fear. How would she ever have the courage to stand up and dance and swirl her skirts, much less giggle and make eyes at gentlemen? As she chided herself internally she was surprised by Madge approaching her in a businesslike fashion.

"Josephine, I would like you meet Mr. Harris." Madge said, indicating a very fat man standing rigidly behind her.

Jo looked up and saw the fat man gazing at her hungrily. She recovered from her shock well enough to stand and smooth her dress, attempting a smile.

"How do you do, Mr. Harris?" She managed to squeak in his direction.

He licked his rubbery lips lasciviously and leered at her. "Good, good," he said in a high-pitched voice, "yes, she is just what I was looking for."

Using all her strength to keep her contempt from showing on her face, Jo again nodded while looking at Madge to see what to do. Thankfully Madge was quite adept at dealing with girls new and uncertain. Taking Jo's hand, she guided it to Mr. Harris's arm and gave Jo a little shove toward the staircase.

"The boudoir at the top of the stairs is very pretty, why don't you show it to Mr. Harris, Josephine?" Madge said confidently.

Mr. Harris jauntily pulled Jo toward the stairs as she breathed deeply to quell her shaking knees.

Once inside the soothingly decorated boudoir, Mr. Harris sat on the edge of the bed and removed his hat, looking at her expectantly. Remembering Juanita's words of advice, Jo asked him about his day.

"I'm not interested in conversation!" He snapped, "I travelled a long way and want to simply have my needs met. What is it with women always wanting to talk? My wife is bad enough."

And with that he began the rather difficult task of unbuttoning his large coat. Jo moved to help him but he just waved her away. His large size made movement arduous and she could hear him breathing heavily, sweat beginning to drip in little streams down his forehead. She stood helplessly looking at him as he hung his coat over the footboard and began working on his vest.

"Well," he snapped, "aren't you going to remove that dress so I can see your young body?"

She started in surprise. Of course, the other girls had prepared her for this. Their dresses were not as difficult to remove as many of the dresses in fashion that season with their clasps and buttons. She reached around and unhooked the few hook and eye closures and stepped demurely out of her white frock. She carefully picked it up and folded it over the other side of the footboard, trying not to shiver too noticeably in her corset and pantaloons.

Mr. Harris, now freed of his shirt, was sitting in just his breeches at this point. He looked her over appreciatively. "Yes, now I see why Madge wanted so much for you, you are beautiful. Well, sit over here and get to work!"

Jo did as she was told, keeping her face passive and her words polite, though wanting to scream in disgust at his rudeness and sweat. He was, thankfully, easy enough to please. Juanita was correct in her direction that once she could get his thing out of his pants it was easy enough to take care of the business at hand. Jo had carefully inserted a Pessairre as instructed and was prepared to endure the pain some of the girls said was inevitable the first time, but Mr. Harris seemed uninterested in anything more than being stroked and fondled. Jo was able to keep her britches on throughout the ordeal, no small blessing, considering how much she disliked the entire situation.

However, Mr. Harris seemed unaware of either her discomfort or tension, and after he had groaned and finished in pleasure he leaned against the soft pillows and immediately started snoring. His pants were still around his ankles, but Jo decided she didn't want to run the risk of waking him so she covered him loosely with a blanket before quickly pulling her dress on and scurrying out the door. She took a few moments in her own small room she shared with Liza, cleaning up in the small basin, before heading shakily back downstairs.

Though it had gone well, she supposed, she decided a young girl definitely needed a little more conversation and guidance before being left with a man. Shuddering at having to do it again, she held her head high. This was not a choice, this was what she had to do. Walking bravely down the stairs, she kept her beautiful face still and calm, hiding the fear and sadness beneath the surface.

Chapter Six

Mr. Wolfe

Though Josephine never could be said to enjoy her unchosen profession, she did learn to endure it. Thankfully, most men were much more pleasant and polite than Mr. Harris and were thrilled to have such a rare beauty as Josephine at their service. She quickly learned how to help them undress, and how to make light conversation to ease her own tension. She became skilled at flattering and coaxing them into a comfortable position, helping to make the entire ordeal pass as quickly as possible while still providing the service the men were paying good money for.

In this way two years passed quickly for both Josephine and Liza. They grew more and more bold, enjoying the personal freedom and material wealth it gave them. Any given evening Dutch Jo could be heard in the parlor gaily singing and laughing, as the gentlemen admired her great beauty. Liza's cheer and wit attracted a great number of gentlemen. They surrounded her as she regaled them with stories and jokes. Liza learned to drink whisky with the men, throwing back to or three glassfuls in an evening before heading upstairs with her intended patron for the evening. Men clamored for an evening with Liza, knowing she would perform tricks other ladies might not be willing to perform.

Josephine, being Liza's close friend and confidant, became privy to these tricks of the trade too. Though she was less exuberant and cheerful about employing scandalous techniques, it became known that she, too, had some prowess in the boudoir. Unlike Liza, Josephine was disciplined and serious. Her use of skilled service was for a reason, like everything she did: to make more money.

Liza spent nearly every dime she made on expensive gowns, fancy perfumes, and jewelry. She did not see the need to save, no matter how many times Jo tried to convince her it was not only necessary but vital. Liza would just laugh her carefree laugh and change the subject.

Josephine, on the other hand, saved everything she could. She became a skilled seamstress as a matter of necessity since she rarely purchased any new clothing, choosing instead to mend and create her own. She did not join the other ladies when they drank whisky, or travelled out on town to eat in fancy restaurants, or take in shows. Instead she hid all her cash in a secret hiding place in the bottom or her dresser. Josephine had plans.

But Josephine soon caught the eye of a gentleman. The evening started like any other with the girls dressing in their rooms, talking and laughing and telling stories. Josephine was wearing an elegant silk dress in a becoming robins-egg blue which set off her eyes and she was helping Liza to roll her blonde hair into an elaborate upswept hairdo. Jo's own light hair was rolled into a charming chignon that showed off her straight posture and high cheek bones. Both young ladies had been practicing their profession long enough now that they did not feel any anxiety or fear; it was simply another night on the job.

"And then, Mr. Pell rolled over and started to snore...but I was still there underneath him! Ugh!" Liza was cheerfully recounting a recent experience with a customer that few of the girls wanted to spend time with.

Jo laughed, "You are a good sport for taking him on. I'm not sure why he thinks he wants to always go upstairs. He should just save his money if all he needs is a nap! But if he's here again tonight, I'll take him. That Oscar Tate was sure looking at you last night and he is a good tipper!"

"Thanks friend, I appreciate it. Actually, I think Madge should make Olympia go with Mr. Pell, she's new. He'll be a good start for a new girl. Boring, to be sure, but a nice way to ease into it."

The two friends were still giggling about previous clients as they sashayed into the main parlor. At first, Jo didn't notice Mr. Wolfe, he was just another gentleman in the parlor after all. But after she had made her way to her favorite settee near Francis and his piano she felt eyes burning into her. She looked up and saw there was a new blackjack dealer. He looked down bashfully as soon as he realized she had sensed him looking, but she was used to men and continued to stare at him with confidence. At this point, after working in a bordello for over two years, Josephine had no shyness preventing her from connecting with any man who interested her. And this man interested her.

She supposed it could be that he was not there as a customer and therefore posed an actual challenge. But it was more than that. His large frame, deep brown eyes, and heavy brow gave him a scary look that contrasted with the gentleness rippling just under his surface. He sat at the blackjack table with confidence, dealing cards to the gentlemen surrounding him, but clearly trying to avoid raising his eyes and having to meet the unwavering gaze of Josephine.

Josephine had grown confident in her ability to attract men using just her large blue eyes. She knew now the power her beauty held over men and she enjoyed wielding it, especially when the man wasn't quite certain he was ready for her. And for whatever reason this man was not prepared to be with her.

Then she saw why. A solid, confident woman strode into the room and stood just to the left of the new blackjack dealer. She spoke to him and he nodded, murmuring something back. So, he had a partner and, most likely, wife. This was a new situation at the St. Louis Hotel. Madge and Francis had only recently installed the blackjack table and it had proven to be very popular, though finding a reputable and skilled dealer had not been as easy as they had first believed it would be. Their initial dealer had indeed been talented, but had lacked ethics, disappearing on his third night with all the profits. The second dealer had lacked any dealing skill and had ended up angering their customers. This new dealer, however, had a truly professional air about him, as did the strong woman next to him.

Jo dropped her eyes from the handsome man. She respected women; in fact, she would never attempt to make another woman's life difficult. Though she was aware that many of her clients had wives who would not approve of their husband's visit to her boudoir, actually attempting to lure a man away from his wife was a completely different scenario and Jo would not even entertain the notion. She pushed the man out of her head and turned her attention to other parts of the room.

But somehow, his presence in the room continued to attract her, despite her intentions of ignoring him. She could feel his gaze throughout the evening as she visited and sang. It didn't take long for his wife to start to notice too, and before long Jo found herself the recipient of two sets of unwanted eyes. When boring Mr. Pell approached her she practically jumped up and dragged him up the stairs, just to escape the obvious marital tension between the blackjack dealer and his wife.

The next evening, when she came down, this time wearing her white frock, the wife was there waiting for her at the foot of the stairs. Two gentlemen were across the room reading the newspaper and three ladies were sitting comfortably around the room, no one paid them any mind.

"Well, how do you know my husband?" She demanded without even so much of a hello.

"Excuse me. I'm not sure I know what you mean." Jo demurred, though she did. She decided her best tactic was unwavering politeness.

"My husband, Benjamin Wolfe, your new blackjack dealer? I will not endure him being seduced by a harlot like you!" The woman spat out.

Jo took a deep breath and stepped past the woman with a slight "Excuse me." She walked across the pretty parlor toward her favorite purple settee and sat down elegantly. The woman hurried along behind her.

"Ma'am, I am sure I do not know what you are talking about. I do not know your husband and you have nothing to worry about. I do, however, know men. And if you are interested in keeping this husband of yours I would suggest you put this jealousy under wraps. He is working in a brothel."

This speech, so forward and truthful, spoken with such confidence from Josephine, that it gave the woman pause. She stared back for just a moment and then seemed to redouble her efforts at being angry at Jo.

"Well, he may be working in a whore house, yes, but no other whore seems to interest him but you. So, if you know what is good for you I suggest you keep your distance!" And with that, she turned on her heel and flounced out of the room.

Shaken by the strangers pronouncement, Jo sat up straight and looked across the room at her friend Olympia who couldn't have helped but to have heard the whole thing.

"What was that all about?" Asked Olympia, joining her. Her sweet freckled face was wrinkled up in worry.

"I have no idea," Jo said, shaking her head, "the new dealer's wife seems to think he and I know each other and she wants me to stay away from him. Not a problem!"

But it ended up being more of a problem than she had anticipated.

For the next month, Jo did stay away from Mr. Wolfe. Though she did find her eyes straying to him, and on occasion she felt the electric shock of accidentally meeting his penetrating gaze as he was trying not to look at her. His wife, still standing next to him as they worked always noticed, sending Jo evil glares while her husband tried to look away from the beautiful blonde.

But one evening, Mrs. Wolfe was not there. In her place was a younger version of Mr. Wolfe, possibly his brother. Josephine tried to pretend she did not notice, but there was a brief involuntary swell of anticipation as she realized he was not with his wife. Her gaze travelled to him more than usual that night as she cheerfully visited with patrons and other ladies. Lately she had been singing more and more with Francis. Her sweet voice was often requested by patrons who loved to listen as well as watch her sing. As she was singing a sad ballad about a lost bird that her mother had sung to her, she let her eyes drop for just a moment toward him. He was gazing at her with his head cocked to the side, a look of sweet joy on his face. Jo did not care for propriety, she finished the last two verses just gazing into his eyes, singing only to him. She was beyond worrying what other patrons thought of them.

When she finished she started, realizing where she was. She retired to her settee and turned to visit with Liza.

"What is happening between you and Mr. Wolfe?" Liza asked with a smile.

"Nothing! Not anything at all. I have never even spoken to him."

"Ha! The man is clearly in love with you. Too bad he has that jealous shrew of a wife to contend with. I heard how she threatened you earlier."

Jo shook her head, she could rely on the girls to freely share any gossip amongst each other and this wasn't something she imagined would go unnoticed.

Just as she was about to whisper more of the detail to Liza, she felt a hand on her arm. She looked up to see Mr. Wolfe, looking down at her tenderly.

"Miss. Josephine, could we please have a moment?" He asked, his voice deep and calm.

She rose and took his offered arm, unsure what he expected of her. Did he intend to go upstairs to the bordello? No wonder his wife was jealous! But no, he led her across the room to a quiet spot near the library where he indicated two chairs where they could speak away from the noise and music of the main room.

"I suppose you may wonder why I have been so forward, staring at you so impertinently." He began, smoothing his shiny hair back nervously.

She smiled and nodded, though she had already imagined he shared an interest in her as she did in him.

"You see, I believe we traveled here on the same boat. Did you come with your parents, about five years ago, on a boat from New York?"

Jo's mouth opened in surprise. He did know her! His wife was right! But how did she not know him? Jo could only nod in astonishment.

He leaned toward her eagerly, causing her heart to beat more quickly as she caught his strong masculine scent. His knee just brushed hers and she found herself gazing at his lips as he explained how he had been on the same boat.

"I was fourteen at the time, recently orphaned. I was just a boy, much smaller and underfed. My brother and I worked on the boat to pay our passage. I was climbing the rigging and adjusting sails all day, every day. I would..." he swallowed, looking down briefly. His usual confidence briefly shadowed. "I would watch you as you moved about the deck with your parents. Your beauty is uncommon, your mother was very beautiful too. I heard they have passed away. I am sorry."

Jo found her voice at last. "But why did you not tell me before this evening!" She finally exclaimed.

"I - I couldn't. My wife, she was so jealous. She could sense somehow, in that way wives do, that something was going on inside. And when I wouldn't tell her - how could I tell her how I watched you from above? How could I tell her how I admired you? How could I tell her how my heart sang when I saw you enter this parlor all those months ago? But she knew."

"Where is she tonight?" Jo managed to ask.

He shook his head, "I'm not sure. She met with our banker this afternoon to go over our accounts and never returned. I...shouldn't talk about her. I will only say that her father was the Captain of the ship I worked on to gain passage here. He took a liking to me and arranged our marriage before she and I ever met. She has been a fine wife, respectful and polite. She may not be affectionate and her temper can get in our way, but I have no complaints.

"But I wanted to explain to you, tonight while she is not here to feel badly about us speaking. I knew you had noticed my impertinent staring and I needed to clear the air. Forgive me."

And with that he stood, adjusted his hat, and returned to his table.

Jo felt dizzy with the information. Try as she might she could not recall Mr. Wolfe on the boat, the entire ride was a blur to her. It had been the last time she had been with her parents before they had fallen ill and died and she didn't like to think about that time. She sat still for some time, just thinking about the information, wondering what to do with it.

The next evening, Mrs. Wolfe was again not at her husband's side. This evening, however, he was pale and shaky. Halfway through the night his brother, who had again accompanied him, had to take over the dealing and Mr. Wolfe left abruptly. Josephine wondered what had happened. For the next week, Mr. Wolfe was at work with his brother and he seemed withdrawn. Though he did not leave again, it was as if he were not really there. He barely spoke as he worked the table and left immediately upon counting out his chips at the end of the night.

The ladies spoke of the strange situation as they dressed to work, speculating as to the location of the sour-faced Mrs. Wolfe. They didn't have to wonder for long. Madge, never a proprieties to let gossip or rumors run her establishment, leaned her head down the hall and hollered down at the ladies.

"Mrs. Wolfe run off with their banker, she did! Left poor Mr. Wolfe on his own. I never did care for that unhappy woman. But it looks like we've got his little brother as a second so we're fine around here. Now quit your fretting ladies and get down there. We have a group of cowboys just up from Wyoming and I imagine they have some extra cash for a lively girl or two."

Josephine was surprised at her own reaction to the news that Mrs. Wolfe was out of the picture. Jo had never formed any type of true connection with a gentleman, though there were plenty she enjoyed and preferred to work with. But there was something about Mr. Wolfe's gentle confidence that kept and held her attention. But as she always did, Jo kept her feelings to herself, hiding her emotion behind her pretty face before entering the parlor.

For the next two months, Jo and Mr. Wolfe exchanged pleasantries, meeting up each evening in what was becoming their customary spot by the library to visit about their respective days. He gradually lost the pallor that had struck him upon learning about his wife's sudden departure and she lost the uncharacteristic nervousness his presence gave her. As time passed, their brief exchanges became more intimate. Soon they were sharing their hopes and dreams as he held her small white hand, though they had yet to venture upstairs.

Yet, she was still a working girl and he did not acknowledge any pain when another gentleman would reach out to her and lead her upstairs as he was working his blackjack table. But Josephine was acutely aware of his gaze following her as she walked up the stairs to work. She was even more aware at the coldness he tried to hide when she returned afterward, slightly richer but hollower in her soul.

Because though Jo and Mr. Wolfe shared what they pretended was a friendship, they had never declared any feelings of love for one another. He was awaiting paperwork for a divorce and seemed to want to do things correctly; she was still just a prostitute who had no claim to any other life until she could save enough money to pull herself to another situation.

Until one January evening, Mr. Wolfe entered the parlor later than usual. He strode in with a confidence surpassing even his usual ease and walked right up to Jo, who was standing near the fireplace talking with Olympia and Liza.

"I need you," he said to Jo, reaching for her hand. Jo could feel her friends exchange a gleeful glance, they were often teasing her about her 'beau'.

Laughing lightly, she began to walk toward their usual spot by the library.

"No." He said, tugging her gently toward the stairs. "I need you." His eyes were burning as he stared deeply at her with an ardor that took her breath away.

Without a second's hesitation she took his hand and led him upstairs to the last boudoir, the most elegant. He grabbed her by the shoulder just as she shut the door and spun her around pulling her close and looking down into her eyes.

"I love you Miss. Josephine. I have loved you since you were eleven years old and I watched you on the boat. As of this afternoon I am a free man." He got onto his knees and extended a small silk box, open to reveal a large diamond ring.

"Will you marry me?" His pleading eyes, looked up at hers and she smiled and nodded.

"Get up! Get up Mr. Wolfe - Benjamin. Of course I will marry you." She helped pull him to his feet and watched in awe as he placed the ring on her finger. Then he held both her hands, leaned over and kissed her.

For the first time she led a man to the bed and felt desire burning through her. This was not something to get through and sneak out afterward but instead something to savor and enjoy. Removing their clothes was a pleasure, as was kissing each part of his body as it was revealed. Better yet was seeing his eyes travel over her body as she showed it to him, bit by bit, finally allowing him to taste and touch her. She thrilled when he touched her, looking deep into her eyes. This was what it felt like to actually enjoy her work, heart and soul!

Josephine and Benjamin Wolfe were married soon after in the nearby courthouse, her closest friends including Liza, Honoria, and Olympia, were in attendance. Benjamin was happy to bring his new bride to their own spacious apartment near the elegant Saint Louis and even happier she did not have to work in her previous profession again, though she did still meet regularly with her friends. He continued to deal blackjack at the Saint Louis, eventually investing in the business and acquiring part ownership along with his friend Mr. Sterling. He brought Jo with him on occasion during the day so she could visit her friends and on special occasions to sing or dance and work alongside the proprietress managing and guiding the girls.

In this way, life passed by in a flurry of joy and peace, especially with the arrival a few short years later of their daughter Clementine. Josephine and Benjamin were thrilled with their little family and jokingly planned to have many more children and grow old together surrounded by grandchildren. But nothing lasts forever.

One spring evening, Josephine accompanied Benjamin when he went to The Saint Louis. Josephine was going to sing for the birthday of an important politician. After leaving Clementine with their trusted nanny Ruby, Jo began her evening by discussing the vocal arrangement with Francis. Marriage suited her. The years preparing delicious meals for her husband had allowed her to fill out in a pleasing way and she now wore her flaxen hair arranged softy around her face in the latest upswept style.

Jo still enjoyed regular visits with Liza, Honoria, and Olympia who continued to work at the hotel. Francis still played the piano, gaining a wide popularity even though he never wanted any type of fame. Jo would meet with her friends early in the morning for a walk or a visit in the kitchen to catch up on the latest gossip. There were more and more difficulties in San Francisco with the city government beginning to crack down on parlor houses.

Madge had decided she had endured enough and had retired, taking a small apartment nearby. The new proprietress, though a reliable partner for Josephine and Benjamin, wasn't as helpful as Madge had been.

Madge had always encouraged them to enjoy the finest travel and entertainment when they took time away from their work. She would regularly take the girls to nearby fields and mining camps on beautiful days so they could get a change of scenery. The ladies felt lucky to work for their previous employer. Anabelle, the new proprietress, was more concerned with the government and kept them under more strict control. She did not want any of her ladies to leave the house, they were discouraged from traveling, and they no longer visited nearby fields or mines. Worst of all, when Liza had complained, Anabelle had told her to move to another place. Mr. Wolfe immediately countered with his promise of fair protection, but Liza was insulted. For Josephine, there was an even bigger threat: an elegant house of French demimonde had recently opened just across the street and the competition was beginning to affect everyone. The Gold Rush was winding down and the money was not flowing in as it had been before. Josephine and Benjamin were looking for ways to help their business.

On this April evening, as Jo was just beginning to sing her second song of the evening, she looked across the room at her dear husband. He looked up from dealing cards and she smiled at him. She was reminded of their first days together, of how they had met, and her smile grew broader. She thought of their sweet daughter, who had recently lost her first tooth, and of what a wonderful father Benjamin was. Josephine scanned the crowded bar, it was a well-attended birthday party with many of the most prestigious citizens in San Francisco in attendance. Near the blackjack table, the guest of honor, an important politician, was exclaiming boisterously while puffing away on a cigar. Just as the politician was getting up to request another drink there was a deafening pop then another. Jo stopped singing and looked about in confusion, seeing a tall thin man with a mustache standing not five feet away pointing a pistol toward the politician. The gunman, seeing two large men walking menacingly toward him, sent off two more shots toward the blackjack table before turning and fleeing. He didn't make it far before the men grabbed him and pulled him out the door.

Through the ensuing pandemonium, Josephine quickly made her way toward the blackjack table. She wanted to get Benjamin and leave as quickly as possible. But when she arrived she was pushed back by a line of men who were surrounding not just the fallen politician but what appeared to be a second body on the floor next to him. It took Jo but a moment to comprehend what had happened.

"No!" She said softly, pushing past to get a certain look, but even before she saw his pale face she knew: her husband was also dead.

Not waiting, not speaking a word to anyone, she pushed back through the crowd and out the door onto the dark street. Taking deep breaths to try to calm herself, she shook her head to try to shake the image of her beloved husband on the floor in a pool of blood. But it would be burned in her mind forever.

Chapter Seven

Decisions

Josephine grieved by staying busy. Clementine, who at seven was just old enough to understand that her father was gone, was a loving support. The two clung together for comfort. But mainly Jo made plans. She and Clementine remained in their cozy apartment downtown. Benjamin had not come from money but his time working as a blackjack dealer and their shares in The Saint Louis had allowed them to live comfortably. Jo was able to continue to provide for her child, though she knew eventually her savings would run out. Life was more difficult without Benjamin, but she was getting back into a regular routine. Until things got even worse for her just six months after her husband's death.

Josephine and Clementine were just returning from a walk to the nearby greengrocers where they had purchased two pumpkins. Though they were both still grieving, they were trying to continue with life by taking part in fun activities like carving jack-o-lanterns for All Hallows Eve. But as they crunched through the fall leaves toward their brick building, Clementine pointed up toward the roof of their building.

"Mama! Look!" She cried.

Josephine was horrorstruck as she saw their apartment engulfed in flames. Already surrounded by spectators, some just staring others breaking windows and beginning to loot the clearly hopeless building, Jo watched helplessly as her home went up in flame. Holding her young daughter close she allowed them just one short moment to watch before pulling her child away from the ghastly sight. It would not be long before the entire building was gone. As they stumbled back up the block toward The Saint Louis Josephine wondered how she would ever recuperate from this set back.

Josephine quickly realized she did not want to stay in The Saint Louis with Clementine. The French parlor house across the street would only gain in popularity as more and more actresses and working girls won their country's lottery to immigrate. Jo spent the next three days quietly plotting and planning how she could provide the best possible life for her daughter. Her gentle beauty hid her shrewd intelligence, but Jo had spent the past nine years observing life in hotels and parlor houses and she was beginning to plot a plan.

She brought up the subject first with Liza, Honoria, and Olympia.

"Ladies, what if I could offer you a better life than here at The Saint Louis? Would you take it?" Jo asked her friends as they braved the cool fog while on their morning walk.

The girls laughed and immediately asked Jo what she meant.

"I'm gathering a group of people to travel to the new gold country - in a town called Lewiston. The California gold is beginning to dwindle, but miners are just beginning to find gold up north. I am making travel arrangements to travel by steamboat up the Columbia once the spring thaw comes. Once there, I will open an elegant parlor house. I need experienced, elegant ladies like you. And I will only take the customary 15% plus room and board."

Liza didn't even need to think about it, "Yes, Jo, I'll go. My mother gets more and more burdensome everyday. I need a change of scenery. San Francisco is beautiful but I've been here long enough. Lewiston? Sounds like an adventure!"

Olympia and Honoria needed a little more time. They had a few more questions about how they would get there, how long the travel would be, and what type of town they were moving to. But after thinking it through they were also happy to say yes.

Josephine spent the next few months making preparations. She sold her share of The Saint Louis. She arranged for travel on a steamship to Portland, Oregon then booked passage on a smaller steamboat traveling down the Columbia River to Lewiston. Within days she had gathered seven more beautiful and experienced women besides Olympia, Honoria, and Liza. Plus three musicians including Francis, and she had persuaded an old friend, Roy, to join them as bodyguard as well as Clementine's nanny, Ruby, a patient older woman who had retired from the working life. The allure of a new gold rush was enticing and her new recruits were eager to begin their new adventure.

Though Josephine had many fears and concerns about bringing little Clementine on such a great journey, she knew she was doing the best she could to provide a better life for her daughter. She extracted a promise from not just Liza but also Ruby, Honoria, and Olympia that if anything were to happen to her they would care for Clementine as if she were their own.

Liza, always an optimist, laughed. "We're just going up north, Jo! Don't always worry so much!"

Jo decided maybe Liza was right, this could be the adventure all of them needed, Idaho Gold Country - look out!

Chapter Eight

The Columbia River

By the time Jo and her girls arrived at Portland her nickname Dutch Jo, could be heard on everyone's lips. Though her stern scowl reminded people she did not like the name, it still stuck. Mainly because of her slight accent, left over from her childhood in Germany, along with the strong leadership she quickly demonstrated as she took charge of her ten ladies left the sailors and passengers on the S.S. Pacific in awe. Despite her youthful beauty, Josephine commanded respect and she kept her ladies under close watch the entire trip. Clementine, carefully guarded by Ruby as well as the entire company, enjoyed the novel sights and was soon comfortably exploring her surroundings. The ladies, too, were enjoying the beauty of the open landscapes and ocean views as well as the elegance of traveling without having to work every night.

Not that a few gentlemen did not try to engage in their services! Though Jo insisted on complete discretion and her ladies were of the highest ranking women of a certain virtue, it was still unheard of for so many lovely young ladies to travel together without husbands or fathers to watch out for them. Josephine had anticipated that the sailors and single gentlemen on the steamship would try to get free services from her young charges and she had given them firm instructions on how to best deter unwanted advances. Of course, not all advances were unwanted, and by the time the ship had arrived in Portland Jo and the girls had already brought in considerable income. As they traveled north, they saw fewer and fewer women and Jo could see that her entrepreneurial brain had led her in the right direction.

No travel can be expected to go entirely smoothly and the next leg of their journey proved much more interesting. As they boarded the Colonel Wright, the new stern-wheeler that would carry them to Lewiston, Josephine was surprised to see six other girls boarding the boat ahead of them. These fair-haired young ladies had been standing on the dock in Portland, their rosy cheeks bright in the cool morning air.

"Jo, it looks like we might have some competition!" Liza whispered into her ear, indicating the line of young women leaning over the railing after they had begun moving out of the harbor. They were all fresh-faced and innocent, dressed in demure, brightly-colored cotton frocks. Josephine and Liza were standing nearby, trying not to appear to be looking at them.

"Well, first they are not that much competition for us, Liza. They are clearly very young and inexperienced. Would you look at those expressions?" Josephine gave her friend a rare smile, reassuring in her lack of concern.

It was true, the girls were chattering excitedly amongst themselves in what seemed to be German, gesturing wildly at every new thing around them. They were unaware of Liza and Jo on the other side of the deck. It seemed they were new to this county and did not have the worldly air of true working girls.

"What are they saying?" Liza asked, aware of Jo's sensitivity to her accent but also close enough to her to be able to address her ability to speak German.

"The boat is noisy, but it sounds like they are really interested in the birds." Jo laughed, "sorry, I know that isn't very interesting. I also heard them saying they needed to practice dancing and that their employer expected them to be in their room by 8:00 tonight. I think they are being closely chaperoned. Just like we are closely monitoring our girls, right Liza? No unexpected events?"

Liza and Jo, along with Jo's bodyguard Roy and the three male musicians, Francis, George, and Winthrop had kept an eagle eye on the girls. With so many bachelors aboard the S.S. Pacific and now again on the Colonel Wright, the ladies had received a lot of attention. But these new fair-haired beauties were an interesting addition to their sailing party. The mystery was soon solved as an older couple and three younger men joined the ladies, looking over them protectively.

"Daughters?" asked Liza.

Jo shook her head, "No, I doubt it. They are all too close in age. They are more than likely a little friendly competition for our business, but not to worry. We have our skills and charms, these young miners won't know what hit them! No sweet-faced little German girls are going to take away our customers."

And with this cheerful proclamation she walked boldly to the older couple, extending her hand in a confident greeting. Liza was soon joined by Olympia, Sally, and four other ladies from their party, Ida, Honoria, Emblyn, and Roseanna.

"Leave it to Jo to get right down to business!" Sally said, watching the little scene on the other side of the deck.

Emblyn, adjusting an elaborate ribbon over her blonde curls, looked at the new girls with interest. "I don't mind a little competition, there certainly are enough men to go around!"

Roseanna smiled in agreement, "Besides, it would be fun to hear where they are from."

Ida was looking at the three large young men standing nearby, "Yes," she added, "and they can probably introduce us to their handsome chaperones!"

They could see Jo, her face unreadable, as she nodded, listening to the older gentleman. He was a large, ruddy-faced man with a full mustache, his wife was equally round and rosy, but she appeared to be much quieter than her husband. The three younger men standing just behind them, visiting solemnly with the young girls, were also large, though not one of them looked able to grow as impressive of a mustache as the older gentleman. The young gentlemen seemed entirely unaware of the young women standing with them and were instead gazing back intently toward the elegant ladies across the deck.

Olympia and Ida were deciding whether or not now would be a good time to practice their eye-attraction technique or if it would prove too effective and make it hard to get rid of these young men. As experienced working ladies, they had developed many effective strategies proven to attract and please gentlemen. One of the simplest and most fail-proof was the eye-attraction technique. It was Liza who had given it a name, though many of the ladies had come up with the final details through practice. The trick, the ladies had decided, was in remembering 5-7-5: the lady needed to make eye contact with her selected gentleman from across the room and hold the gaze for five seconds...then quickly look down for seven seconds...then look back at him for five seconds more before looking away completely. The gentleman would then be snared and could soon be counted on to approach the lady.

Before Olympia or Ida had a chance to try this out on one of the large young gentlemen, Jo returned.

"Did you see our cabins yet, girls?" Jo asked cheerfully as they leaned against the white balustrades of the upper deck. The sternwheeler was picking up speed as they moved down the Columbia River, Jo held her hand over her eyes as she gazed toward the rising sun. The view up the Columbia River Gorge was impressive, a novel sight for each of them. The endless water, evergreen trees and enormous river led to wilderness the ladies had only heard about but had never before seen.

"Yes! Jo they really are beautiful," Ida bubbled eagerly, "tiny little compact spaces with absolutely every comfort of home. Our four bunks fold down and our window opens on top to let in fresh air."

Jo seemed pleased at the description. She led them down toward their rows of rooms, explaining about the young girls as they walked. The girls were dancers from Germany and the older couple and their three sons had employed them to work for the next year in a new saloon they would be starting just outside of Lewiston. The ladies were all said to be virgins who would not, under any circumstances, be allowed to be alone with any gentleman. They were to be employed for a year to pay their passage from Germany. The gentleman, his name was Hans Stohlhofen appeared to be a strict employer, but honest.

Ida kept looking back toward the younger gentlemen, earning some gentle teasing from her friends.

"Which one are you looking at, Ida?" Laughed Sally, "Don't think we can't see you making your eyes at those poor German boys. They won't know what hit them! And with a strict father like that - you might be wasting your time!"

The trip down the mighty Columbia started well and all the ladies were really pleased with their accommodations. Though it was March and quite cool, they quickly settled into the routine of walking along the top deck for fresh air conversation. It wasn't until the third evening, when they pulled into a small harbor called

Wallula Landing one afternoon, when things got interesting.

Up until this point, the sternwheeler had chugged along comfortably, providing a soothing backdrop to the now customary walks around deck, the shared meals in the dining cabin, and the gentle rocking sleep in their cabins. The male passengers had begun to move beyond politely tipping their hats as they walked by to making polite conversation with the ladies as they leaned against the deck railing or relaxed while watching the scenery of the Columbia River Gorge change from deep green trees to bare brown hills as they got further from the ocean.

Ida had wasted no time in using the eye-attraction technique on the tallest of the German brothers, easily enticing him to approach her and request a walk. Under the watchful and suspicious eye of Jo she joined him, though their intimacy had not extended past stilted conversation as she held his sturdy arm.

Honoria, too, was spending her afternoons walking with one particular gentleman, a young cowboy who was with a group of men continuing to Walla Walla to work at the Fort. John Perkins had been traveling steadily west with his parents most of his life, having been born in a small cabin in Missouri. He had left his parents and sisters behind in Portland to seek his fortune in the booming Walla Walla country and was full of enthusiastic tales about Indians and construction; he had been commissioned to help build the road from the Fort to the town. Honoria, who had worked only a short while at the Saint Louis, was transfixed by his ready smile and colorful stories. His steady cheerful chatter reminded Honoria of her older brother, Reynaldo, who had been killed while fighting in the Mexican-American War, when she was a small child.

Honoria's dark eyes sparkled as she listened and walked, causing her friends and employer to watch her carefully. On this third day when the Colonel Wright pulled near the sandy beach at the junction of the Columbia and the Snake, Honoria was again walking along the deck with her young gentleman. Both she and Mr. Perkins were much more subdued than they had been the previous few days, they were talking in quiet voices as he prepared to disembark. His coach was being loaded and he and some other passengers were going on to Walla Walla. As he was leaning to give Honoria's smooth brown cheek a tender kiss, a soldier wearing the distinguished navy and yellow of his regiment, rode up and gave a friendly wave.

"You might want to wait until tomorrow when the sun comes out and melts the ice before continuing up." The soldier could be heard calling to the first mate.

Captain White emerged from his tower and climbed easily down to the young soldier who was now standing next to his horse, speaking with him seriously. Both shielded their eyes from the setting sun while looking down the Columbia toward the Snake, gesturing and shaking their heads. Finally the soldier turned to his horse as the captain climbed back aboard. The soldier finally caught sight of the many ladies in their fine dresses leaning agains the railing watching the proceedings. His eyes widened and his mouth opened in surprise as he realized the boat carried beautiful women. Nodding his head while tipping his cap he backed clumsily into his horse, causing the horse to whinny and move away and the ladies to titter. His smooth face reddened, but his obvious glee at seeing a boat full of women seemed to outweigh any embarrassment he might feel. Tipping his hat once more before pulling himself onto his horse, he galloped back the way he had come, toward Fort Walla Walla.

Captain White was shouting quick commands to his crew, who had sprung to action. From what the ladies could hear, there was ice just up the river and they would be staying the night here at Wallula Landing. Before the captain even had the opportunity to finish his preparations and come down to speak to Josephine and other important passengers to relay the information a great whoop could be heard from the direction of Fort Walla Walla, just over the hill. A band of soldiers on horseback was approaching at great speed, yelling and waving their hats. Two of the German girls, whom Jo's girls had by this time ascertained were the youngest and named Amalie and Willie, shrieked in terror at the approaching mayhem. Olympia covered her mouth in fear and Ida hid behind her tall German beau. But within moments it became clear that this was not a gang of angry warriors or hoodlums sent to attack their ship; these soldiers were happy. And when they saw the same soldier as before, this time in the front seeming to lead the pack, it was quickly understood that he had gone back to tell his friends that ladies were at Wallula Landing and would be for the evening.

A brave young man with a full chestnut mustache hopped spryly from his horse and swept his cap from his head with a great flourish, smiling up at Josephine as she stood on the upper deck.

"Welcome to Wallula Landing, Miss!" He called out cheerfully, "my young officer here informed me there were some young ladies on board the Colonel Wright this afternoon and I can see this happy news to be true. I am Captain Mullan and my men and I here have been working all winter to build roads and secure our fort. We would most appreciate the gentle company of elegant ladies such as yourselves."

Josephine nodded solemnly, acknowledging his polite greeting. Turning back toward the Captain and Hans Stohlhofen Josephine leaned in and had a brief conversation with the two gentlemen. Captain White nodded and could be heard to say, "Yes, as long as nothing scandalous happens and everyone pays for their drinks I don't see why not."

Stohlhofen said gruffly in his thick German accent, "Yes, my girls can dance. This will be good advertisement for my business. But under no circumstance shall any type of improper conduct take place."

Captain White turned back toward Captain Mullan, "Hello Captain, it is always a pleasure to see you! The ladies would love to entertain your men while we wait for the ice. It is my pleasure to invite you and your men to a party here on our boat this evening. If you, sir, will come aboard we can discuss the specifics before they join us."

While the two captains and two business owners discussed the logistics and financial arrangements of such a large party, the ladies worked together with the crew to decorate the dining hall and upper deck. Clementine was reluctant to go to bed, but Ruby cheerfully led her to the elegant cabin she shared with Josephine. The ladies were able to procure a dozen hanging lanterns from the storage hold and Josephine had two rolls of beautiful red ribbon, which they draped along the balustrade, giving the ship a cheerful and festive feel when the first men started to pour on board later that evening.

Chapter Nine

Frozen at Wallula Junction

Wiping sweat from his brow, James Shaw continued walking behind the two oxen as they seeded the fertile Walla Walla valley soil. James had been seeding his family farm for the past twelve days and his body, though aching, was stronger than it had ever been in his 24 years. The Shaw family had traveled west via wagon train ten years before and their ranch was now one of the biggest and most abundant in the valley. James had farmed alongside his father and uncles since the spring they had arrived, though this year he was overseeing new workers. His mother had died the previous spring, the day after the baby had arrived, and his father had traveled to La Grande to negotiate the sale of more farm land, leaving James alone with his grandmother and three younger siblings. His two younger cousins, Calvin and Raymond, were here on this day to help finish up the last of the seeding.

James was the rock of his family. Though he often thought of his mother, he knew his siblings and grandmother relied on him to be strong about her loss. James had taken on the role of singing to the younger girls each night before bed, something their mother had done for him and his younger siblings. Before his brother Joseph had died in the plowing accident two years before, both boys had often teased their mother when she would sing to the younger girls. Now that both Joseph and mother were gone James sometimes ached as he sang 'Mocking Bird' or 'All the Little Ponies' to his sisters. But he sang despite his breaking heart, because he knew it was a way to keep his sisters connected to the mother and brother they had all lost too soon.

Especially Clara, the baby, who had lost her mother after only one day and who would only know about both her and Joseph through stories.

On this early spring day James was looking forward to finishing up with the seeding, taking care of the oxen, and returning to the homestead to finally rest after preparing the fields for the growing season. He knew he really only had a few days before the demands of the ranch continued to call him, but he was glad to be done with this portion of the job. As he was unhooking the two large animals, his friend and neighbor Edward Jennings came riding up, his blue soldier uniform making him look older than his 22 years.

"Jimmy!!" Edward practically yelled, uncustomary for the mild-mannered boy, "Jimmy! You have to finish up, get cleaned up! There are ladies up at Wallula Landing!"

James pushed his straw hat back and looked up at his friend.

"Ladies?" he asked in his slow, easy way.

"Yes! A whole slew of them! Pretty young ladies in fancy dresses on the sternwheeler from Portland. Even a couple with yellow hair." Edward was grinning from ear to ear as he thought of the bounty of ladies on the boat.

Edward was the son of the livery owner in Walla Walla, a cheerful and talkative boy who loved horses. He had recently signed on with the army regiment stationed at Fort Walla Walla and, to his mother's great relief, he was spending the majority of his time laying stones to build the road connecting the fort to the town 35 miles away. He and James had been friends since earliest childhood, not just as neighbors but because the Shaws were frequent customers at the Jennings stable in town. Now that they were older Edward occasionally stopped by for James so they could spend an evening at one of the local saloons when he had a free day.

"I'm just headed home to smarten up," Edward called over his shoulder, "I'll pass back by for you when I go back to Wallula. You better be ready!"

James smiled and said he would be, laughing at his friend's exuberance. Neither young man had much experience with the fairer sex, having grown up in a town that was considerably dominated by soldiers, miners, trappers, and traders. Though both had younger sisters and there were a few young women their own age, Walla Walla had decidedly slim-pickings for gentlemen of a marrying age. The few families who had brought daughters over the Oregon Trail were extremely protective of them, as both Edward and James were of their own sisters. James had never been alone with a woman who was not a relative and he didn't know what he would do with himself if given the opportunity.

But it wasn't something he was going to miss out on.

An hour later, the two young men tied their horses off with nearly 100 horses at Wallula Landing, looking with awe at the large stern-wheeler, twinkling with candlelight on the water. Loud laughter and jaunty music could be heard from inside.

"Do we dare approach?" James nearly whispered, looking nervously at Edward.

Though Edward was younger and appeared at least as nervous as his friend, he feigned courage he did not have. "Heck yes we do! Let's go!"

Just as they stepped toward the boat they heard the pounding of hooves behind them and five more gentlemen rode up, these were all considerably more nicely turned out than either the young rancher or the soldier, though they were friendly despite the obvious disparity in their wealth.

"Well hello Mr. Shaw and Mr. Jennings!" The oldest of the group called as they slid from their panting horses. It was a local merchant, Mr. William Smith who was accompanied by his younger brother. Oswald Kelly the wealthy and handsome mining outfitter as well as Andrew Milner and Caldwell Rogers who owned the newly erected mill also greeted them as they approached.

The seven men from Walla Walla soon joined the crowd thronging the boat, as eager as the soldiers and other local gentlemen to get a glimpse of the ladies dancing onboard. Everyone was prepared to empty his pockets, but James had decided before they boarded that he would simply stand back and observe. He was feeling shy of approaching a lady, especially these sophisticated ladies, until he felt someone staring at him. He turned his dark eyes toward the the back of the galley where the band was playing a lively number and he saw a flaxen-haired beauty gazing intently at him, her blue eyes locking on his. Just as he registered what was happening, she looked down, her eyelashes lowered in a demure way he found endearing. He studied her slender neck and smooth cheek and was thrilled when she looked up again, this time smiling a small smile before looking away.

His heart gave a lurch. He had never seen a more beautiful girl and he had to speak to her. Without regard to anyone around him he began pushing toward her, unaware of the music or dancers or anyone in his path. Within moments, he was by her side and had his hand in hers. He was so overcome by emotion for this lovely woman he couldn't think of what to say, but he remembered the love he had felt for his own dear mother and how, as a young boy, he had touched her cheek and how his mama had always laughed.

Without giving it one thought, he reached his other hand toward her, stroking her cheek with a tenderness he never knew could spring from his hands, so accustomed was he to driving animals and fixing machines. But this woman inspired poetry in him and he wanted to sing to her. She looked at him in surprise, her blue eyes snapping gaily in the candlelight.

"Well! Aren't you the forward one!" Emblyn exclaimed, surprised by his large size, but even more so by the softness of his touch.

Realizing how foolish he must appear, James stepped back and shook his head. "Please forgive me, I was overcome. You are everything a woman should be, I..." he trailed off, wondering if he was just making it worse. Then he realized he was still holding her hand. He looked foolishly down at it, so smooth in a white glove, so tiny in his large calloused hand. He looked back up at the lovely girl and was relieved to see her laughing.

"Maybe we should take a short walk?" She asked, her confidence and mirth putting him at ease.

He extended his arm toward her and within moments they were nearly alone on the sandy beach just outside the boat.

Chapter Ten

Roseanna

Roseanna was older than the other girls, though she had moved around enough to avoid becoming known as an old-timer. She was beginning to see traces of age in the corners of her eyes and backs of her hands, but her olive complexion hid her age well. Roseanna had developed as a woman quite young. She had been a working girl since the age of 12, deciding it was better to live amongst other women and get paid than be forced into something by her mother's unkind husband in order to avoid injury.

As a very young girl, Roseanna and her family had lived in Boston and had enjoyed a certain amount of comfort. Her father had worked in a shipping yard and her mother had cared for an elderly woman of great financial means. Roseanna, her parents, and her younger brother Reginald had lived in a small, pretty cottage behind the great house of the older woman and life had been pleasant. Roseanna and Reginald had accompanied their mother to see Mrs. Donway each morning, sitting with her as their mother prepared meals. Mrs. Donway had been kind and had taught both children to read and appreciate literature and poetry. Because the elderly Mrs. Donway was losing her eyesight, she would ask Roseanna's mother and, later, Roseanna, to read to her. Tennyson, Hawthorne, and Shakespeare became her friends and mentors as she sat quietly alongside her mother and brother enjoying the beautiful and sometimes enigmatic words.

Life in the Mrs. Donway's house was a pleasant escape from the silent anger permeating their small cottage. Roseanna learned to shut out the angry accusations and suspicious glares her father directed toward her mother by cowering with young Reginald, repeating stories and poems from their elderly benefactor. When her father would come home smelling sweet and swaying, asking more loudly than usual what his wife had done all day, she knew to quickly grab her brother's hand and pull him out the door. Even if this meant sleeping under the awning of the roof to avoid his cobra-like wrath.

But when Roseanna was 10, Mrs. Donway had passed away. It was an easy passing leaving her simply cold one morning. But not an easy passing when their family found themselves turned out of the only home the two children had known. The Donway manor sold and the profits divided between Mrs. Donway's two faraway children. From one week to the next, Roseanna went from a life of comfort and learning to one of fear and uncertainty. Her mother, to this point always reliable, took to crying silently as they made their way from one tenement house to the next, looking for a place to live or work or both. Her father grew quickly angrier and more unstable, blaming her mother for their lack of housing.

The first night without shelter, the family had taken refuge with the only family they had in Boston, their mother's cousin who lived near the river with her husband and four young children. They passed a humiliating and miserable evening sleeping on the floor, creeping out the next morning in the pre-dawn with a whispered thank-you and no breakfast. The cousin watched them go with pain in her eyes, clearly wishing she could help, but barely surviving herself. As their father stomped off to the shipyard that morning, leaving Roseanna, Reginald, and their silently-sobbing mother standing alone on the street with one box holding their possessions, he did not even look back. None of them were surprised when they did not see him again.

Thankfully, it was late spring and they were able to sleep outdoors taking shelter near an abandoned building, carefully avoiding others who had clearly been homeless for a long time. Roseanna tried to keep her mind full of the literature she had heard, the cheerful poems, the tragedies much worse than this, in order to remove herself from the terrible situation. Their mother proved industrious, finding employment in a large clothing factory where she worked sewing ready-made clothing. They were able to move into a dirty tenement building, Roseanna and Reginald did not even mind the rats they could hear scuffling through the walls because they were so relieved to have shelter once again.

For a brief time, it seemed their lives would be satisfactory, Roseanna and her brother walked with her mother to the factory each morning. They then visited the new part of the city they were now living in, learning what they could about the opportunities surrounding them. Other children were attending a public school located two miles from the tenement, Roseanna and Reginald, remembering the pleasant days listening to poetry and literature, pressed their noses against the gate, watching the nicely dressed children enter the brick building.

"Don't worry, Reggie," Roseanna promised, "I will find a way for us to go to school."

But she hadn't. Within months, their mother had brought home a man, a sullen and unsmiling man named Mr. O'Leary who served as her supervisor at the factory. When she first brought him home one evening, without warning or explanation, both Roseanna and Reginald were concerned. Was their mother being supervised at home too? Would she lose this job also? But no, Mr. O'Leary seemed only interested in eating the meager meal their mother bustled about to lay before him, ignoring the children almost entirely. Almost. He had taken Roseanna aside one time to brush his hand down her slender back, as she walked by to take his plate.

"You are growing up too, aren't you?" He had asked, nodding appraisingly at her. "Soon you will be able to come work for me in the factory."

Roseanna hadn't known how to respond and when she looked at her mother, her mother only gestured for her to work more quickly to serve Mr. O'Leary.

Reginald had not minded Mr. O'Leary, in fact Roseanna felt betrayed by her younger brother as he talked to the sour-faced man, greeting him as he came into the house. Mr. O'Leary quickly became a fixture in their small home, leaving Roseanna feeling stifled as he watched her with his beady eyes. Although Roseanna attempted to speak to her mother on some of the few occasions she found herself alone with her, her mother only brushed her off with irritation.

"Oh Roseanna, don't you understand I need to have a life of my own? Mr. O'Leary is helping us, don't you see?"

Roseanna tried to see. She did see that Mr. O'Leary did occasionally bring food, even meat, but this did not make his more and more frequent unexpected grabs to her hip or back any more welcome. Roseanna found herself staying as far from her mother's male friend as possible. But this proved more and more difficult, especially when her mother arrived home one day and announced she and Mr. O'Leary would be getting married. Roseanna crumpled, tears springing to her eyes.

"Mother, he is not kind to me. Please." Roseanna said softly.

"Roseanna!" Her mother snapped, her eyes flashing, "how dare you try to put a damper on my one chance for happiness!"

Roseanna knew she was defeated. She tried to find ways to avoid being at home, and she soon got her wish. When she turned 11 a few weeks later, Her new step-father declared she was old enough to begin working in the factory.

The factory was miserable in nearly every way: hot, stifling, hard to breathe, few breaks, the incessant whir of sewing machines, the constant threat of being let go for even the most minor infraction. If it hadn't been for the other working girls Roseanna would have never made it.

In particular Roseanna made friends with Kathryn Barry, a cheerful redhead who had travelled by herself from Ireland at the age of 14. By herself! Kathryn, who insisted in her good-natured way on being called Katie, also lived in the nearby tenements. She shared hers with two other girls who also worked at the factory. She saw in Roseanna someone who needed guidance and quickly took her under her wing, giving her advice and friendship in a way no one else ever had. In return, when Katie discovered Roseanna knew how to read she begged her for lessons.

"You can teach me and we can really make something of ourselves!" Katie told Roseanna as they walked home after a long day of work.

So it was that Roseanna began the not easy task of teaching an uneducated Irish girl about letters and sounds and fitting it all together to make words. Each morning Roseanna would bring a dog-eared piece of paper with a new lesson written in cramped letters below the previous lesson and she would explain as they walked. As they returned home in the evening she would explain again. During their 20 minute lunch, they would sit together and practice a little more. It was slow, but Katie was picking it up. She was bright and eager, but the lack of books surrounding them as well as their crushing work schedule made mastering the task difficult. But they stuck at it.

When Mr. O'Leary was passing out the paychecks for Roseanna's first pay period, he passed his step-daughter by as if she were not even there. She watched him in disbelief, unsure what to do. Katie did not allow this to go by without comment.

"Did that horrible man just jilt you?" Katie asked as she folded her check before tucking it into her apron.

Roseanna felt a pain deep in her chest as she nodded. What was she going to do? This work would be unbearable if it weren't for Katie, but to do it for free was slavery! And she lived with the man and his hands were getting busier and busier, never letting her pass by without an aggressive pat or tug.

Katie shook her head, "I've seen what he does to you. That man is going to destroy you and your whole family in more ways than one. I've seen it happen before. I think you need to go to Mrs. O'Laughlin."

Roseanna looked at her in confusion. Mrs. O'Laughlin was well-known around the factory, many girls spoke of her as someone who helped them. But Roseanna had yet to understand how she helped or even who she was.

"What do I do? How do I find her?" She asked her friend.

"I've only heard, in fact I've considered talking to her myself." Katie said enigmatically as she pulled on her coat. They were clocking out and walking toward the door to leave. Roseanna began pulling out their daily reading lesson when Katie stopped her.

"No, today we should go see Mrs. O'Laughlin. This is serious and all the girls say she can help. She can give us a better life. My roommates? Bertha and Mary? They went together to see her last week and now they are considering they may no longer even have to work here. And... they are both making so much they are threatening to move to a fancier apartment. They can't believe I haven't gone with them yet."

Roseanna stopped walking, other girls leaving the factory walked around her as they hurried toward their homes.

"This sounds almost too good to be true, Katie. Be careful," she said, looking closely at her friend.

"Come with me! Your step-father is not a good man. He is making you work for free...and the way he looks at you is - not right. I had a neighbor that did things to me that I don't like to think about. He started that way too."

Roseanna was not entirely sure what Katie meant, but she knew Mr. O'Leary's grabbing hands were not a good thing. And she knew she was nearly powerless to stop it and it terrified her.

But she did not feel like going to see a strange woman named Mrs. O'Laughlin would help her situation. Telling Katie good-bye she went the opposite direction from her friend hoping her mother would help her appeal to her step-father at home.

But things at home did not go as she had hoped. When she approached her mother about the missing paycheck, her mother had only sighed tiredly and shaken her head.

"Oh honey, you are so expensive to house and feed. I'm sure he will give you some money for your work eventually."

And that had been that. Roseanna wanted to scream. She wanted to fly at her mother and demand she help her, demand she give her the kind of care she had given before their lives had fallen apart and they had lost their home and Mrs. Donway and her father. But seeing her mothers defeated face, she only turned silently and said nothing, retreating to her room to read a book she had managed to procure by trading her lunch with a well-read floor manager.

And it went on like this for the next three pay periods, her step-father never acknowledging his theft or her slavery and her mother quietly accepting it. Worse, Katie had arrived at work the next day with a glow of excitement chattering on about Mrs. O'Laughlin and how she lived in a beautiful apartment building and she had arranged for Katie to start working as an "escort" beginning the following Friday. Katie would be paid five dollars. Five dollars!

"But what will you have to do for five dollars?" Asked Roseanna.

Katie had shrugged, attempting not to look nervous, "I asked Bertha and Mary and they told me it isn't too bad. You just talk and laugh and make sure you are having a good time. That's all the gentleman wants. And five dollars! That's almost double my weekly pay, just to spend an evening with a gentleman."

At the thought of five dollars Roseanna felt her heart sink. Her own money, sitting in the evil O'Leary's pocket, was burning a hole in her heart. Feeling a swell of rage Roseanna looked up toward Mr. O'Leary's office where he sat, more than likely, with his feet up surveying his charges while he did nothing at all.

"Join me if you want," Katie was saying to her young friend, "Mrs. O'Laughlin said she has more gentlemen than she knows what to do with and they enjoy the company of young ladies. So if you get tired of this let me know. Bertha and Mary have already left this factory, six days a week in this stifling heat is just too much! I may not be too far behind them!"

With that, Katie turned back to her machine before the floor manager could come down and reprimand them for talking. Roseanna continued with her work too. She had to do something, this was not right. If her mother would not help her she would confront Mr. O'Leary herself.

When the whistle blew for lunch she did not go toward the small break room with the other girls, instead she went toward the back office where Mr. O'Leary closed himself off during the day. Her fury was enough that she gave a more forceful knock than she had intended and stepped inside with a straight back and determination that he immediately recognized as one of a girl demanding her rights. He smiled, ready for a challenge.

"Yes?" He asked, looking her up and down in a lecherous way she found uncomfortable.

"I am here for my paycheck." Roseanna said, proud of the strength of her voice.

He leaned back and laughed, "But you, my dear, already received it," he said smoothly.

She felt the indignation color her face, making her voice higher than she had intended. "No I have not! You do not hand me a check when you hand out the rest!"

"Ah, but young Roseanna, I allow you to eat and live under our roof. This is more than enough payment. If you want money from me there are things you can do." He looked at her intently, then rose suddenly striding toward her.

She tried to back up but was already to near the door. He was quickly upon her, grabbing her shoulder and turning her around, shoving her towards his desk. Before she could make a sound, he pulled her skirt up, revealing her homespun cotton pantalettes. He began tugging them down as she struggled and began to holler indecipherably.

"Come on now," he said, his voice low and panting, "don't struggle, it just makes it worse. This will only take a moment." She continued to claw her way away and yell gibberish as she felt his hands on her bare thighs.

Just then she saw, out of the corner of her eye, the door swing wide open.

"Get off her! Get off her now! Help! Come quick!"
It was Katie, hollering in her loud Irish brogue, screaming down the hall and then returning.

"Roseanna, get up! Are you unharmed?" Katie's concerned green eyes looked her over carefully as Roseanna adjusted her clothing. Mr. O'Leary had run from the room almost immediately.

"We need to get out of here. Now!" Katie said urgently, grabbing Roseanna's hand. "He will make this our fault, a theft or...something. Come now!"

Before Roseanna even had a moment to think about any of it, she was out the door and down the street, running toward the unknown apartment of Mrs. O'Laughlin. Before the week was done Karie had arranged for both herself and her young friend to live in a small room in the basement of the building. It was not perfect but a vast improvement over the tenement and completely safe from any further mischief from Mr. O'Leary. After seeing her friend safely navigate the new business Mrs. O'Laughlin offered, as well as the excellent pay, Roseanna eventually took part herself.

From that point on she and Katie worked together, always knowing where and when the other was working, prepared to step in to help if necessary.

Roseanna was able to teach her friend to read and the two became well-known for not just their beauty, but their intelligence and understanding of literature and poetry. They soon began to laugh at the idea of charging a mere five dollars for an evening! Regarded as two of the most highly-sought after courtesans on the east coast, both Roseanna and Katie could fetch as much as fifty dollars for an evening of fine dining, the symphony, and their illustrious company. It did not take long for men to begin propositioning marriage. Roseanna, remembering her own useless father and even worse step-father, always declined. Katie, however, was finally persuaded by a steel mogul, and at the age of 26 retired from service.

Once her friend had settled into a comfortable life of domesticity, Roseanna decided to seek out a new adventure. Hearing of the gold rush in San Fancisco she had booked passage west. She had settled comfortably into a new life as a working girl moving from various elegant hotels in the city. She eventually ended up at The Saint Louis Hotel, a respectable San Francisco parlor house. She enjoyed her work. She enjoyed the comfort, the power and control she held over men, the money she made, and the beautiful dresses. But as the years went on, she began to long for peace, she wondered if there might be more to life than just parties and lively conversation. She began to imagine a life with just her books, and a few loved ones. So when her friend Josephine approached her about heading north to Lewiston, she didn't even hesitate. She once again packed up her beautiful belongings and set out toward a new gold rush. But this time she was with a whole group of beautiful and lively fun ladies.

Chapter Eleven

Mr. Shaw and Emblyn

As they walked, James Shaw found he could speak more easily to Emblyn than he had ever spoken to anyone, soon revealing his grief over the loss of his brother and mother, his inability to show his family how he felt, and the fear he might fail at caring for them. She, in turn, was able to share some of her life with him. How she had travelled with her family on a wagon train to California, full of hope for a better future, only to lose them to one tragedy after the next as they encountered hunger and illness along the way. How she and her mother had tried to survive alone after her father was shot in a raid, cleaning and cooking for wealthy families, before her mother fell sick and left Emblyn alone at only 17 years old.

She tried to stay cheerful, this wasn't a story she normally shared with potential clients. She knew gentlemen preferred a cheerful, lighthearted lady, and Dutch Jo had arranged for this evening as a presentation of sorts to the gentlemen of this valley as to the delights that would await them in Lewiston. Emblyn knew it was her professional duty to stay optimistic and not talk of such desperate times, but somehow James brought out her vulnerability and she trusted him. As they walked through the cool spring air, his wool coat draped over her shoulders, his arm keeping her steady, she felt she had found a long-lost friend. Her years of worry over daily survival, her loneliness at losing her family, her shame at the profession she had no choice but to enter faded away as she shared and listened with this young man.

They were both surprised when the sky began to turn the faintest shade of pink and the first songbirds of the morning began to sing. They looked at each other and laughed, they had been talking and walking all night! James, being familiar with the territory, led her back toward the boat and had her to her cabin door before the sky was completely light. In the early morning silence he reached up and touched her cheek once more, this time without any hesitation.

"I know this is abrupt Emblyn, and we have only just met, but I feel I love you. Will you marry me?" He spoke firmly and without hesitation.

Emblyn felt tears spring to her eyes as she looked deep into his. Without waiting a beat she responded with an enthusiastic yes.

Leaning in to give her a loving kiss, James promised he would arrange for a preacher before they ever even reached his house.

While James and Emblyn walked the night away, the rest of the ladies also enjoyed the beauty of the night. The girls had all pulled out their finest gowns and jewels and had outdone themselves with elaborate hairstyles. The many weeks they had been traveling had been full of interesting sights and the occasional flirtation, but this opportunity to see so many eager and free-spending men was energizing. It may not be conventional, but this was going to be a party to remember!

Honoria and her cowboy were thankful for the extra time they had been given, they could be seen leaving the boat together and strolling along the sandy beach beneath the newly budding trees, holding hands. Ida too was not deterred by the newly arrived soldiers or the merchants and ranchers from nearby Walla Walla that were beginning to come over the hill as they heard about the party, she too, remained intent on her Johan, her new German acquaintance. The rest of the ladies, though, were nearly overwhelmed with the sheer number and variety of gentlemen streaming onto the boat.

Hans Stohlhofen proved to have an aptitude rivaling Josephine's for making money and the two of them quickly established a system where gentlemen could pay for incrementally more exposure to the young ladies. Simply being on the lower deck was the least expensive option moving up through seeing ladies dance and being near the musicians that were playing cheerfully on stage all the way to paying for three-minute personal dances and walks along the upper deck. Both proprietors were thrilled with the outcome of this unexpected delay.

Josephine was relaxing for a moment during a rare lull in the excitement of the evening when Liza approached her and made a suggestion.

"We need a grande finale Jo!" her friend suggested, her eyes shining.

Josephine nodded in agreement. Frances had taken a break from his superb piano playing and was imitating Mark Twain to the great delight of the crowd. The ladies were dispersed throughout the room, talking to groups of three and four men each, captivating their audiences.

"Well," continued Liza, "remember the time Hilde, that Gypsy girl, worked at The Saint Louis and she taught you one of their traditional dances?"

Josephine reddened slightly at the memory, she had been 16 at the time and Mr. Wolfe had been in attendance, as had his wife. Jo had created quite a stir in the parlor that evening; her husband had often requested variations of the dance when they were alone together throughout their marriage.

"You could do that tonight!" Liza announced, her voice carrying as Frances completed his routine.

Olympia, Ida, and Roseanna were close enough to hear and all three turned to see what their friend Liza might be suggesting to their employer. Olympia graciously moved away from the three young gentlemen who had been fawning around her and approached Josephine and Liza asking what Jo might be considering. Ida, Julia, and Roseanna were not far behind.

When Liza explained her idea all three were equally eager to see the performance. Though Jo rarely performed since getting married, she was well-known as a talented and fiery dancer. Before she could offer any protest the band had been informed and a gypsy number was beginning. Jo confidently moved to the center of the room and began her sultry dance.

The gentlemen watched in hushed silence as she sliced the air with her hair and serpentined her hips and shoulders to the exotic music. She removed her silky red scarf, using it to shield her eyes then her mouth in a blend of passion and raw emotion that left more than a few masculine hearts beating faster than usual. By the end the crowd erupted, begging for more, but Jo only laughed and returned to her place by the door.

Mr. Stohlhofen, not to be outdone, moved to the stage and surprised them all by bursting into an opera no one quite recognized, yet everyone felt they may have heard before. His voice was clear and his notes were precise and by the time he was done every person on the boat felt they had magically stumbled upon the best party they might ever attend.

Chapter Twelve

Mr. Kelly

As Roseanna took a moment to observe the party, she felt all of her 32 years. She had always been careful to conceal her age, keeping quiet about her history. But being at this party this evening was beginning to wear her down. She looked across the deck at all her friends, full of vigor, dancing and laughing in the moonlight. Roseanna had watched Josephine dance with a smile, thankful to be with such an elegant madame. Though she didn't know Jo's age, Roseanna knew she was still older and wondered how long she would be able to keep up the life of late nights and entertaining. With a sigh, she moved over to the railing of the sternwheeler and looked out across the moonlit beach. She smiled as she saw Emblyn walking slowly with a gentleman across the tree-lined grass.

"It's a beautiful night, no?" One of the many men who had been surrounding her all evening smiled down at her. He had a round, kind face and wore a distinguished top hat. What was his name? She smiled, realizing she was working and her reverie could cost their establishment the reputation of being full of fun and lively girls. No gentlemen were going to seek out the company of sullen, pensive ladies!

"It certainly is!" Roseanna exclaimed gaily, tossing her head and gazing up at the moon. "I love it here already."

Three other gentlemen, all equally distinguished in various top hats and waistcoats clamored at her every word. Roseanna had mastered the art of entertaining gentlemen. She was well known at the many houses she had worked in for her charm and wit and had often coached younger girls in conversation and decorum. But if she thought about it, which lately she had been, it exhausted her. She longed to sit in silence with someone with whom she could simply feel at peace.

It was at this precise moment, as this one momentary ache of desire crept into her consciousness, that she happened to look behind the throng of top hats to see a man with an intelligent twinkle in his bespectacled eye. He was looking at her not with the admiration and longing of most gentlemen, but instead with cheerful amusement. He seemed to see right through her. She wondered how long he had been watching her and who he was.

The band struck up a lively number and the round-faced gentleman asked her for a dance. She politely accepted, easily sliding into one cheerful polka after another as the men who had paid the price took turns dancing with her. It was when the band struck up a romantic waltz, however, that the gentleman with the knowing gaze approached her.

Bowing politely before taking her in his arms, she was struck at how well she fit. He had a soft velvety voice, but he spoke with confidence when he first addressed her.

"Good evening, I am Oswald Kelly. You certainly are a talented conversationalist," he said with a smile. "You seem to be able to speak with ease about any number ideas these gentlemen bring up."

She nodded demurely, looking up at him through her eyelashes, a practiced move that never failed to elicit even further admiration from her clients. Though for this gentleman she was more interested than usual. He seemed to exude a quiet intelligence that she found intriguing.

"But," he continued, "what are your interests? What would you be conversing about, if you could choose?"

Roseanna nearly stopped mid-glide as she contemplated this unheard of question. Her interests! Never had a man asked this simple question! She had enjoyed admirers who had favored her, showering her with gifts and attention. She had even had a few who had been interested in her life, though she had always suspected an ulterior motive. But this was a new phenomenon indeed.

"I - I love to read." She admitted, her usual vivacious charm now subdued by the vulnerability she felt at admitting her greatest love.

"Literature?" He asked, looking deeply into his eyes.

She nodded. "Yes, and poetry. Anything, really, but I have been enjoying Charles Dickens of late. Also the poetry of Longfellow and Browning, so intriguing."

She stopped speaking, realizing she may have said too much. But he was gazing intently at her, his eyes full of admiration.

"You should meet my mother. She was a school teacher in New York before my father and I moved her here to start our mining outfit."

"Your mother?" She regained enough composure to contain her laughter. Gentlemen did not introduce their mothers to ladies of the night!

"Yes, she loves literature, in particular Browning. She always read to me, though I prefer the cheerful accounts of Twain myself. In fact, mother has given me an appreciation for all of the finer things in life - music, visual art, even dance. I suppose it is a good counter to the rough life I lead as mining outfitter."

Roseanna was intrigued, she wished to speak further to him and the waltz was nearly done. She knew a good number of men were lined up, hoping to dance with her, but she decided to run the risk of disappointing Miss Josephine and suggested they take a stroll on the deck.

He seemed surprised when he readily agreed. He led her onto the deck and before either knew it they had passed the rest of the evening in pleasant conversation. They had moved from literature, poetry, and music to their personal histories, hopes, and dreams. By the time Mr. Stohlhofen and Miss. Josephine were pushing the gentlemen off the boat both Roseanna and Oswald felt they had know each other forever.

"Roseanna, I would like to bring you home to meet my family."

She nodded, almost unable to speak. Although the first time he had mentioned this idea she had found it comical, now she understood that his family was so important to him that this was a serious idea.

"No, Roseanna, I mean now. I would like to bring you home as my wife." He got to his knees and looked up at her. "Will you marry me?"

She found herself laughing and agreeing immediately, pulling him to his feet. Although she had received many offers, this was a man who suited her intellect and she knew he would be a good husband for her.

"Will you take me to a preacher immediately?" She asked him, smiling.

"Anything! I will do anything for you!" He declared, sweeping her into a large embrace.

Taking her hand, he led her toward the entrance to find Josephine to inform her that she would be losing one of her best girls.

Chapter Thirteen

End of the party

Josephine was not unaccustomed to her ladies being swept away by infatuated gentlemen, though to lose two in so short a time was not something she had planned for. As she and Mr. Stohlhofen were encouraging their visitors to leave the boat and their ladies to retire to their rooms, Josephine spoke to both Emblyn and Roseanne.

"Yes, I will give you my blessing," she said kindly, "but only if you understand that you may never return to me. If he is not as honorable as he claims to be in this evening of passion, then I am truly sorry - but I will not be responsible."

Emblyn, her eyes shining with happiness, looked at James standing just a few feet away, his hat in his hand.

"He is a good man! His friend Mr. Jennings vouched for him and I trust him Jo, I do! He said he would arrange for a preacher first thing."

Roseanna, too, looked at her new love, who nodded confidently at her.

"Yes, Jo, I am making the right decision. Walla Walla will be a good place for me to make my home. It is time."

Josephine gave both girls a hug before speaking to the gentlemen about their obligations when they picked them up in the morning.

Mr. Stohlhofen, on the other end of the deck, was having similar conversations, but with less happy outcome.

"No! I will not release them for anything less than $5000 in gold!" He nearly shouted at two young gentlemen standing near the tearful Amalie and Willie.

"Come see them dance when we get established." He said, pushing his two charges towards their rooms where his wife was waiting to guide them inside to safety.

The two potential suitors shuffled off dejectedly, probably trying to decide how they would make it clear down to Lewiston to see the young German girls again.

Honoria was standing on her tiptoes to give her cowboy, Mr. John Perkins one last kiss before he left the boat. They were both somber, but neither was prepared for the finality of marriage. Mr. Perkins had no way to support a wife and Honoria knew that, with her history and his lack of money, the only future they had to look forward to as a married couple was one of misery.

She whispered to him as she hugged him one last time, "Come see me in Lewiston, I look forward to being with you again." Then watched sadly as he joined the rest of the men who were leaving.

By midnight, both Josephine and Mr. Stohlhofen called their girls in and Captain White gave orders that his boat was to be closed to visitors. With many stolen kisses and hopes of seeing the ladies again, the soldiers and gentlemen disembarked, wishing the party could have lasted forever. But the next morning they sailed on - minus Roseanna and Emblyn. Soon they would be in Lewiston, ready to begin their new life

Chapter Fourteen

Lewiston

As the sternwheeler pulled into the mining town of Lewiston, Idaho, the sailors sprang to action around them preparing to dock for the evening. The sun was setting, casting a golden glow over the hastily built wooden buildings and dusty streets, but Josephine was still wary of this tiny settlement where she was bringing her girls. She wondered about her husband's friend and business partner, Mr. Sterling, who had returned from the Idaho Territory full of stories of gold more plentiful than water. He had seen her devastation over the loss of Benjamin and then her possessions and his suggestion of Idaho Territory had seemed a good one. But now, overlooking the few small buildings with wooden sidewalks she had her doubts. The tree-lined Snake River with it's sandy beaches and large rolling hills was impressive, she had to admit, but she hoped Mr. Sterling had presented an accurate depiction when he had told her of the wealth flowing through the area.

Mr. Stohlhofen stood near Josephine and shook his head, "We continue down river one more day, to Orofino. I wish you luck." The two shook hands as Ida gave Mr. Stohlhofen's oldest son, Johan one last lingering look. Though the cheerful and virginal dancing German girls would be just up the river, Josephine and her ladies did not doubt that Johan would be coming to see Ida on occasion.

As Jo and her girls disembarked, followed by their orchestra, bodyguard, and various sailors acting as porters with the ladies' many trunks and personal items, the many men in the street began to stop and turn toward them. Without exception, all were covered with dust and appeared shocked at the sight of so many elegant women. Josephine had arranged accommodations at the one hotel in town, The Luna House, and everyone was happy to arrive and be shown their rooms. Josephine and Clementine shared a large room adjoining a smaller room held by Ruby. The little girl was thrilled to be in the hotel, she loved looking out over the busy street from their second story window. Her mother and Ruby kept a careful eye on her at all times, but loved seeing her exuberant enthusiasm.

The Luna House was the largest building in town and had been recently constructed by the owner, Mr. Hill Beachy. The ladies were pleased to see their rooms were comfortable and well-appointed and everyone immediately began to settle in to their temporary housing. Mr. Beachy was happy to see so many female guests arriving to stay in his hotel, especially because of the number of male customers pouring in after them. The gentlemen began lining up at the Chinese bathhouse across the street arguing to see who could get to the hotel first; many had not seen a lady in months.

They need not have rushed, however, the ladies were tired after their long journey and spent the first part of the evening getting refreshed and prepared in their rooms.

Liza, sponging herself off with scented rose water, called to Sally, who was across the hall. "Have you seen my yellow petticoat? The one with the flowered lace? I think I may have run out of room in my trunk when I was packing, did I put it in yours?"

Sally tossed the petticoat to her friend before asking her to help tie up her corset and button her silk dress.

Julia, next door, asked if anyone had noticed their were no couches in the bar below, "Where do you think the gentlemen will talk with us before we come upstairs? I certainly don't want to have to line up like they do in those terrible places on the row!"

Liza agreed this could be a problem, remembering her mother working in a place like this in New York. "Maybe Jo will just send them up? Or maybe there is a dining room we hadn't noticed. Don't worry, Jo will take care of it.

And she would, in her years married to Mr. Wolfe, Josephine had developed the confidence and manner of negotiating that left no aspect of the arrangement between her ladies and an interested gentleman undiscussed, while at the same time allowing the lady absolute discretion. Only Josephine ever took money, while her bodyguard, Mr. Roy Thomas, watched from over her shoulder. For most arrangements, Jo set one of her sand timers and the girls knew their mistress would be there to knock on their door when the time was nearly up, though for a much higher price the gentleman in question could stay the entire night.

In this particular establishment, Josephine, too had noticed only a few stools and some tables. Her ladies were accustomed to sitting on elegant settees and sofas, though Josephine understood they were in a newly civilized part of the world. But she quickly developed a plan and it proved to be successful.

First, she made it clear that no gentleman would be allowed entrance without paying. She was used to being paid with greenbacks or gold bars in San Francisco, but here in Lewiston Mr. Sterling had warned her that the miners were gathering gold so quickly everyone paid in gold dust. Jo had come prepared with a precise scale and she set her prices based on level and time of interaction.

Next, she directed Francis and the rest of the band to set up at the back of the saloon and to play cheerful music throughout the night. Positioning Mr. Roy

Thomas near the door to the street, she directed her ladies to come down in pairs, to walk prettily around the room, and to speak to the gentlemen she had arranged for them. By the time all ten ladies were downstairs, the first two could discreetly lead their gentlemen upstairs, closely watched by Mr. Thomas. Jo would set the timer before sending the next two up. In this way she could go up to stop the proceedings all at once and the ladies could come back down to start the whole cycle again - if there was time.

The hotel was so crowded with eager gentlemen carrying leather pouches full of gold dust that Josephine was able to charge more for her ladies services than she had ever seen charged in her years of working. It was a busy and very successful evening and by midnight when Josephine, Mr. Beachy, and Mr. Thomas directed the disappointed remaining gentlemen out, Jo's own hidden leather purse was bursting with gold nuggets and dust.

The next morning, Jo was up early and had just finished weighing out gold to distribute to each lady when she received a knock on her door. She stood and walked to her door, opening it a small crack. Mr. Beachy stood in the hall.

"Good morning Miss Wolfe, I trust you slept well." He said, his kind eyes crinkling at the corner.

She nodded, stepping out of her pretty sunlit room into the darker hall. She followed him down the stairs into the warm kitchen, joining him at the small table. She smiled her thanks as he passed her a cup of steaming coffee.

"I wanted to both thank you and warn you. Last night was the most successful evening The Luna House has ever seen, and this gold rush has already brought me profits I never imagined. The business you and your ladies are bringing to my saloon is unimaginable, I am thankful the whisky barge comes this afternoon." Here he laughed.

"But I must warn you. With any gold rush come thieves and bandits. It will not take long for your name to become well known. Last winter one of my friends was murdered as he carried a large portion of gold through the canyon."

Josephine sighed, she too was aware of the danger to be found in gold country. San Francisco had been dangerous for the same reasons, and more, and she had learned to defend herself. She thought of Clementine and her ladies, mulling over possibilities for a better life than this.

"Thank you, Mr. Beachy. I appreciate the honest warning. My girls and I are all protected, we have Mr. Thomas and other means of security."

Mr. Beachy seemed relieved. "Good," he said, "I did not want you to mistakenly think I had the ability to fight off any large men who may take advantage of your situation. I offer what help I can, and you are welcome here as long as you wish."

Jo smiled her thanks before settling in to less serious subjects.

Springtime passed in a flurry at The Luna Hotel. Josephine and her ladies were so popular they were bringing in more money than any other establishment in Lewiston and Josephine was putting her business sense to good use. She had been talking to Francis and Liza, who both had experience in a variety of saloons and hotels to design their own hotel.

"I think it should have a front parlor where they have to wait to be invited in." Liza suggested as she lounged on Jo's bed turning her face to the the warm May sunshine that morning.

Francis sat on the trunk, his silver hair glinting, "I like that idea. I also like the idea of a real stage. Something small, off to the side. Where will you find someone to design the building, Jo?"

Josephine sat at the small writing desk near the window and took careful notes, sketching out plans for potential buildings. Their own hotel had become a pleasant subject of conversation and Josephine was eager to get started on it as soon as possible.

The Luna House had become an important stop for the miners flooding Lewiston and Josephine and her ladies were pleased with the amount of money they were bringing in. They were less pleased, however, with the frequent fighting and even gunfights that seemed to erupt over almost nothing. The evening before it had been in the street right in front of their hotel. Two men had begun yelling about a horse and a saddle and from what the ladies could gather one man felt another had stolen his friend's saddle. It had ended with both men being pulled away from each other as they tried to punch and tear one another apart. The ladies tried to keep their eyes from the windows, but the noise of the fight had been hard to ignore.

Liza was particularly bothered. Though she and Jo were close, she never spoke of her childhood living with her mother in different brothels. Jo had deduced that Liza's mother had traveled with Liza on a wagon train when Liza was very young but that both Liza and her mother had resorted to living in a parlor house upon arriving in San Francisco. Liza, in her flippant and uncaring manner, brushed off any mention of difficulty in her past, but Jo suspected Liza had hidden terrors she did not want to be reminded of. For this reason, at the merest hint of violence, Liza would immediately bolt in the opposite direction and not emerge until everything was peaceful again. Because Liza, with her cheerful banter and quick laughter was so well-liked and sought after, when she disappeared the gentlemen would soon begin asking when she would return.

One evening in early July, an argument erupted down the street from The Luna House. Many gruff and angry voices could be heard coming from the direction of the river and to Liza's horror they seemed to be traveling toward the hotel. Before anyone had time to even look out the door, Liza was gathering up her skirts and ascending the stairs to her room.

When, a few moments later, the argument burst like a cyclone into the saloon itself, the other ladies also took refuge wherever they could, behind tables, chairs, or gentlemen. Josephine slipped behind the bar and pulled her revolver from beneath her skirt, preparing it if necessary.

Two of the men, so covered in dirt only their eyes and teeth were visible, were screaming at a third gentleman.

"You know you poured sand into that gold dust! You were trying to swindle us! We have the dust melted into bars and we showed you the remainder." The larger of the two snarled.

"Liar! I am good to my word, you added the sand if anyone did. I don't owe you nothin' you louse!" The third gentleman hollered.

Before anyone knew what was happening, the third man pulled out a long rifle and shot the suspected swindler dead. He landed in a bloody heap on the floor of the saloon, blood instantly pooling around him.

Honoria and Sally were near the ruckus, trying to make themselves small behind two large miners. Both ladies were pale and shaking. Ida stood frozen near Mr. Thomas, her mouth an O of terror.

The rest of the room stood in horrified silence for what felt like eternity until the larger man said, "Aw, Pete, what'd ya go and do that for? Now they're gonna hang ya!"

Pete looked the most shocked of all, under the dirt and dust his face was clean shaven and his gape-mouth expression revealed his youth and inexperience. He looked around the room, stupefied, as if expecting someone to tell him what to do.

Josephine took charge. "We need to get that body out of here. And does anyone know where we can lock this man up before they decide what to do with him?"

Men sprang to action, moving the body, leading Pete out, and trying to keep blood from soiling the floor any more than necessary. The ladies moved upstairs as quickly as they could get away to talk about the horror they had just witnessed and to get their bearings. Josephine joined them a few minutes later in Sally's room, after ensuring Clementine and Ruby were fine. Her girls looked at her, wide-eyed, as she entered. The music could be heard again coming from downstairs.

"Well, girls, I guess we have no other choice but to get back to work." Jo looked around, "Where's Liza?"

Julia shook her head, "She won't come out of her room. She won't let us go in there either. Something's wrong."

Honoria laughed. "Something is wrong Jo, that man just got shot and killed not five feet from us, and now another man is going to be hung."

Irma shook her head, "And they were fighting over gold dust. Exactly what all of us have sitting in our rooms, unprotected."

"Who's to say we aren't being slipped a little yellow sand in our gold dust?" Asked Fanny, in a worried voice.

Jo held up her hands. "Now ladies, I have thought of these things too. Lewiston is rough. Maybe more rough than any of us bargained for. But we have to stay cheerful and expect the best and we can't just run and hide any time something bad happens. Now, it's early in the evening, do you want to sit up here and cower? Or are you ready to walk down those stairs and go to work?"

One by one the ladies stood and walked through the door. It wasn't until they were all down the stairs that Jo knocked on Liza's door. When there was no answer, she opened it and entered.

The room was nearly dark, the July sun had only recently set and the pink light that filled the room revealed Liza laying face down on the bed.

Jo sat next to her friend and said nothing. After awhile Liza spoke into her pillow. "Is someone dead? I heard that shot, the yells."

"Yes, the right man at least, though soon the other man will probably be hung."

Liza sat up, her normally sparkling blue eyes were dull and she looked at Jo with defeat. "Jo, I can't do this. Lewiston is too rough. The men are pushy and rude. San Francisco could be violent, to be sure, with the thieves and outlaws and card sharks. But this place is full of fights and yelling men."

Jo nodded, "I know. Mr. Sterling was here over a year ago and this is not the territory I imagined I would be bringing you all to work in. I worry about Clementine." She shuddered thinking of her sweet, beautiful seven year old daughter having to continue enduring the daily life here.

Liza just stared despondently at Jo, her face washed in sadness. "We have to do something different Jo." She said solemnly.

Jo agreed, "I've been thinking the same thing. I have spoken to a lot of different men who have traveled throughout this territory and many suggest Walla Walla, just up the river. We were near there when we had that party at Wallula Landing all those months ago."

Liza perked up slightly, "You mean you would consider leaving? I had a gentleman in here last week who had just traveled here from Walla Walla - he had been working on that same road as Honoria's Mr. Perkins. He told me it is an established town with dignified business owners and churches and ranches."

Jo laughed, "You want dignity and churches Liza? Why, so they can picket us when we set up our hotel?"

Liza managed a small laugh too. "I am surprised to admit it, but yes, at least we can rely on a little law and order. No one will be shot or robbed right in front of us."

And just like that, Josephine and her girls were done with Lewiston. Ida, surprised them all by deciding to stay behind. She sent word with her German beau, Johan, in Orofino and the very next day he and his father were at The Luna House to collect her. She had experienced enough of the rough life in gold country. Her friends teased her, saying she would be married by the end of the year. Though she promised she would only be dancing for the Stohlhofen family, the sparkle in her eye gave her away her true feelings for Johan.

Josephine was anxious to move to a calmer and more law-abiding place. She knew she had already given up on giving her daughter an ideal life, she had the financial means and help to be able to shelter her from most of the evening escapades. Josephine herself did not have to engage in the same daily work as her girls and between herself and Ruby, Clementine was well-cared for and protected. However, Lewiston was not an environment that would be good for Clementine or any young girl. It was just too rough. Mr. Beachy was sad to see them go, though he understood. Within a week Jo had arranged for the next sternwheeler to carry them back toward Walla Walla where they would once again begin the first establishment in a new town.

Chapter Fifteen

Walla Walla

Their first view of Walla Walla was enough to put everyone at ease. It was hot, much hotter than any of them were used to since San Francisco had such mild summers, but the trees dotting Walla Walla provided a respite they hadn't enjoyed in Lewiston.

Josephine made arrangements, on the recommendation of Mr. Beachy, for them to stay at a small hotel called The Coast House. The owner was a nervous little man named William Willis, he obviously hadn't been in the company of ladies for a long time and he didn't seem comfortable addressing any of them. He directed his questions to Francis, who would in turn ask Jo.

"Does every lady need her own room?" Mr. Willis asked in his fast, high-pitched voice.

Francis turned to Jo who nodded, a faint smile of amusement on her face.

"Yes," Francis answered.

"For how long?" Mr. Willis asked, now turning to Jo, finally realizing it was indeed this beautiful woman making the decisions.

"We will rent our rooms until we can build and establish our own operation. I apologize in advance for coming in with the intention of being your rival." She said politely.

He was flustered and didn't seem to know what to do with his hands. He stood behind the bar as they made their negotiations, wiping the same spot over and over with a rag.

"No, no, a little honest competition is good for us all." He allowed, nodding rapidly, "I imagine your establishment will be a little different from mine."

Jo looked around at the large, open room dotted with wooden tables and dominated by the long bar. A mirror behind the bar reflected the two large picture windows overlooking Main Street.

"Yes, we run a more intimate, private establishment. Not someplace anyone would simply stop in for a drink. More of a place where people come and stay for a longer visit."

Mr. Willis, understanding her meaning, grew more wide-eyed and nearly dropped the glass he was pretending to dry.

"Intimate?" He squeaked, squirming a little.

Jo looked up at him through lowered eyelashes, "Don't worry about the reputation of your establishment, Mr. Willis, we will maintain our respectability until we have appropriate quarters."

"No, no, by all means, do what you must." Mr. Willis stuttered out, his face now bright red.

News of the newly arrived ladies quickly spread throughout the Walla Walla Valley and gentlemen began to pour into The Coast House. Though the ladies maintained their discretion, there was plenty of money to be made by gentlemen who panned for gold in nearby mines, as well as some soldiers, including Mr. Edward Jennings, who took a break from the construction of military roads, ranchers, and even the respected gentlemen from around town. The ladies even saw many of the same men they had met at their party months before at Wallula Landing. Honoria in particular was thrilled to see her cowboy, Mr. John Perkins, who made his way into the The Coast House just a few days after they arrived. The ladies were all sitting at different tables around the room, chatting with the professional skill they had cultivated over their years of service, when Mr. Perkins walked in.

He stood in the doorway and scanned the room, his stance one of desperation. He was out of breath and it was clear he had just jumped off his horse. Honoria, who was at a table with Sally visiting with Mr. Smith, the owner of the nearby sundries shop, looked up and saw John's eager face. She rose, barely managing an apology to Mr. Smith before stepping toward him. She remembered their friendly conversations and affection on the sternwheeler from Portland. Without a word, she took his hand and led him toward a quiet table away form everyone else.

"I didn't know if I would see you again." He said, stroking her smooth cheek. She smiled and put her hand to his, looking deep into his eyes.

"I'm glad you managed to find me." She said softly, "How is Mullan Road coming along?"

"You remembered!" He exclaimed, his face full of joy. "I was afraid you wouldn't even remember who I was, it has been months and months. But I haven't forgotten you."

She laughed, "Of course I remember you, you are special. I've been hoping I would see you again."

He pulled out a small bag. "I just returned form Idaho gold country. It's true what they say, the gold is everywhere. This bag is full, I have enough I could even buy a little house. Maybe even a little house...for you?" He looked at her with such longing and desire, she felt her stomach lighten.

Yet, she couldn't just answer. She was so eager to be here, to begin this new life. Jo had been meeting with builders and their new hotel would be ready for them all by the following spring. The Coast House, though not as refined as The Saint Louis in San Francisco, was comfortable and the gentlemen came in regularly with bags of gold, eager for company. Honoria was saving most of what she made and she had hopes of possibly opening her own hotel some day. How could she throw this all away?

However, when she looked at John, his soft brown eyes pleading as he looked at her, she softened. He had been so attentive and kind on the boat. The few days they had spent together had been so pleasant, what would it be like to be his wife, to marry him? She considered, finally asking for a day or two to consider. He tried to mask his disappointment, kissing her hand and promising her a good life, promising to shower her with riches.

"Well?" She asked, "What kind of riches are you talking about? Maybe you could give me a little sample tonight? I might have something worth your while."

"Now? Just like that?" He stammered, his cheeks burning pink.

Honoria couldn't help but laugh, running her hand softly over his chest. "Well, yes, now." She leaned in to him and breathed into his ear, "Just like that."

And without another word she pulled him up the discreet back staircase toward her room where she demonstrated just what life with her in his bed might be like.

Chapter Sixteen

Plainfield, New Jersey

Edith Crawford had grown into a beautiful young woman, tall and willowy with long honey hair tied up in an elegant bun. Aunt Agnes had ruled their stately Plainfield home with an iron fist, dictating every aspect of Edith's life. From her music lessons to whom she socialized with, Edith was constantly scrutinized by her elderly aunt. Though Edith was generous and forgiving enough to understand her aunt's desire to give her a good life after the death of her father, Edith still resented the interference. It wasn't until Aunt Agnes fell ill, however, that Edith realized the extent to which she had meddled in her young life.

Edith had missed Liza and Rosie with a deep sadness since the moment she had tearfully watched them walk away all those years ago. She had ached to hear from them, at first in desperation and as time wore on with quiet despair. She had often wondered if they had made it west, even going so far on occasion to send desperate pleas out into the world seeking them. At the age of thirteen, she had sent 'To whom it may concern' letters to all the cities she could locate along the West Coast, pleading with the post master to please reply if he heard or knew anything of her step-mother or step-sister. Even these letters had been mailed surreptitiously, snuck into the post office on the rare occasions Aunt Agnes allowed her to run an errand or visit a tutor on her own. When she had received no reply she had no choice but to wait for the a letter to arrive, but it never did. Now, ten years later, she thought often of her one year living with a sister, but with the resignation that she would never see Liza or Rosie again.

    Her life had been quiet, Aunt Agnes had insisted on closely monitoring her social life, arranging for dignified outings with equally restricted daughters and granddaughters of wealthy friends. Plainfield, New Jersey was a beautiful town where many wealthy New Yorkers settled with their families and Edith was introduced to the most respected and important of them all. Though she formed friendships, most seemed stifled and shallow. She longed for Liza's frank honesty and easy humor, while quietly accepting her fate of a stifled debutante.

When Aunt Agnes fell ill, Edith dutifully cared for her, overseeing the household while spending hours at her aunt's bedside reading the Bible and newspapers. The political strife surrounding, the debate between the states over slavery and the nearby battles were frightening and fascinating and both aunt and niece shared a passion for the subject. But as time wore on, Aunt Agnes faded more and more, leaving Edith to the task of simply ensuring her physical comfort. It was in these last days that Aunt Agnes touched her arm, the elderly lady barely able to open her eyes at this point.

"Yes Aunt, do you need me to get you more water?" Edith asked gently, arranging the coverlet around her small frame.

"No, child. I have a confession." Aunt Agnes spoke in a near whisper, each breath a coming out in raspy gasps.

Edith was confused, but leaned closer to hear the soft voice. "There, there, you can tell me anything. You have always lived a good life." She soothed.

Agnes shook her head slightly, "No, letters. There are letters."

Edith knew, instantly. It came to her without explanation, of course her aunt had confiscated letters from Liza or Rosie.

"From my step-sister? My step-mother?" She asked quietly, trying not to get upset.

Agnes winced, "Forgive me. I wanted what was best for you, I wanted you to make better choices than my brother."

Edith sighed to herself, wanting to speak, but knowing her true goal was to find the letters. She needed to continue the charade of accepting her aunt, regardless of how wrong it felt. "Yes, Aunt, of course. Please. The letters? Do you still have them?"

Aunt Agnes nodded, pointing toward her desk. Edith would never have felt comfortable going through anyone's desk without permission, but with her aunt directing her she discovered a small packet of letters addressed to her at father's house in New York. The house had been sold five years earlier, leaving Edith with yet another chunk of money in her already fat bank account. She wondered if any more letters had arrived there since the sale.

She kissed her frail aunt gently and whispered, "Thank you," before carrying the letters into her own room to read. They started out in Liza's childish handwriting, accounts of her travel over the country by wagon, the tent city in San Francisco, the new hotel with Rosie. Two were from Rosie, short notes in her un-practiced hand, but kind and full of inquiries into her health and well-being. Three others from Liza let her know that, until five years earlier, Liza had remained with her mother at the hotel, The Saint Louis, and was doing well. Though the letters did not specify the nature of her work, Liza intimated that she was doing well financially and earning good money. She described the excitement and wealth of the gold surrounding them, the growth of the new city, and her friends living with her at the hotel. Every letter pleaded with Edith to respond, to let them know how she was faring. Edith felt her eyes well up at the straightforward, cheerful accounts, the concern for her welfare.

Then the letters abruptly ended, at the time the house was sold. Could she go to the house and ask for her letters? Why hadn't they forwarded them on? Had something happened? In a flurry of activity, Edith sent a message to the new owners of her father's house in New York, had they received any letters? Waiting for a reply felt like an eternity, but the next afternoon when one of the servants brought the note into Aunt Agnes' room, it sat atop another small packet of letters. The first few followed the same chatty vein, though both Liza and Rosie were clearly getting progressively more worried about her, asking her to please reply. The last letter, sent six months previously had been from Liza.

July 18, 1860

Dearest Edith

We have arrived in Walla Walla, can you imagine such a name? They just changed it, some of the people wanted to call it Steptoe, but Walla Walla won out.

These parts are chock full of Indians and Walla Walla was one of the tribes, we don't see them though since the treaty. Good thing for that! I'm not as concerned about the natives as I am about all the wild miners, there are some rough fellows out there. They are not such scamps as we saw in Lewiston, everything fell all to pieces there. Luckily Jo got us over here, even though the boys can be wild. Usually they calm right down after a few drinks and good laugh, though, and do they have gold! I have never had so many beautiful dresses, you should see the blue one I just had sent over from Portland!

We are doing well here, Josephine is having a new hotel built, I don't know how that woman does all she does, she talks to the men like she's one of them but she's beautiful too. If you could meet her I know you would love her too. Rosie did not want to come, I suppose it may be for the better, she is slowing down and still has her crotchety ways. I send her some extra eagles with my letters, she needs the money so she can stop working. She is still in San Francisco if you ever decide you want to write. Sometimes I imagine you are not just gone, instead I get the notion you are just ignoring me. Am I just too low down for you? I hope that is the reason you have ignored us all these years. I just hope you are too high-falootin to be bothered with the like of me. That had better be it, you had better be fine.

I wonder if you will ever respond. I just keep writing these darn letters and hope, you will write back, but maybe someday.

Love forever

Liza

Edith chuckled, Liza was still Liza. Full of stories Edith could not ever fully understand and scattered with honest descriptions. What she wouldn't give to see her again! To experience the adventure of living out west, surrounded by all that excitement. She immediately wrote a response to both Rosie and Liza, detailing her life up until this point and sent it on the very next post. She knew it could be many weeks, maybe even months, until it arrived, but she was anxious to make up for lost time.

Compared to Edith's quiet life of directing servants, music, and society obligations Liza's life was like a fairy tale. As Edith dutifully tended to her aunt's rapidly failing health, she continued thinking of Liza and what it must be like to live in a fancy hotel surrounded by cowboys and indians. Edith had secretly been reading what her aunt referred to as "Penny Dreadfuls" for many years, sensational novels depicting the tales of the frontier. Edith longed to experience the stories as she read about Jesse James, Billy the Kid, and Wyatt Earp. Though Edith spent her days speaking in hushed tones to dignified people wearing the finest silks and linens, she longed to tame the wild frontier. By the time her Aunt Agnes had finally slipped into her last peaceful sleep, leaving Edith alone to arrange her quiet funeral, Edith had created an entire fantasy life in her mind about traveling west and joining Liza. Imagining herself riding a horse over vast plains, followed by covered wagons, eating and sleeping near a campfire gave her solace in her time of difficulty. But Edith's life of comfort was too big a draw, and she lacked the courage to set out on toward an uncertain future.

The next few years passed in a blur of pleasant social engagements, parlor concerts, and helping out with the war effort. Edith, at 20 was a lovely woman and had many suitors, but none shared her love of music or light literature and she kept them at a distance. Because of her family fortune Edith often felt that gentlemen sought her company solely to amplify their own accounts. Some were as wealthy as she, such as the dreadfully boring and haughty Mr. Lissander, and she suspected it was his mother who insisted he call. Others, such as the charming and witty Mr. Capshaw seemed to spend money faster than their fathers could supply it and her aunt had warned her to stay far away from this type. Instead, she spent the time she wasn't alone playing the piano or reading or engaging in civil duties and pleasant conversation with any of the other young single ladies of Plainfield. But she was unable to consider any of these ladies as more than a friendly acquaintance, they were all too concerned with moving their way up the social ladder.

She missed Liza and lived for her letters describing her exciting life out west.

She continued to live in her family home, enjoying her beautiful and commodious environment, though she let go of many of the household servants, closing off the empty upper floor. She would have felt lonely in her large home if it weren't for Diana and Sean McArthur, an older couple who had worked for the Crawfords since they had arrived from Ireland twenty years earlier. Childless and dedicated, they were like the parents Edith never had. They had accompanied her from her father's home to Aunt Agnes' when she was a child and she was grateful for their love and support. Edith had often taken informal meals with them in the kitchen when Aunt Agnes was traveling, now that she was on her own she ate every meal in the kitchen. Diana worried about her and attempted to get her to socialize, to branch out into the work of young people around her.

"Edith, it is time you married." Diana urged her gently one evening as they ate a humble supper of stew and cornbread.

Edith, who had spent the day in the garden before perfecting a difficult piece on the piano seemed surprised.

"Not you too!" She said, looking into Diana's kind eyes. "Every one of my acquaintances says the same thing. I am only twenty years old, what would I do with a husband?"

Sean patted her hand, and said in his soft voice, "It would be nice to see you with company, not so alone in the world. You are so quiet and reserved, it is as though life is just passing you by."

"And we are getting along in years, too." Diana added, "What will you do when we are gone? You have no one else and we worry."

Edith considered their words, understanding their concern. "I have Liza."

They both nodded, remembering the cheerful and lively young girl who had been such a ray of sunshine as a child. Edith had never recovered from the sudden departure of her family and they longed to help her find someone who would make her laugh and be lighthearted again.

And so it was that Edith decided to allow an appropriate suitor into her life. Of course she took her time deciding in her own discreet way who it would be. There was Mr. Jones, her neighbor, but she could never get him to talk about anything interesting. And Aunt Agnes had been a big advocate for Mr. Harrison, the son of a banker who had worked with her father, but Mr. Harrison was as shy and retiring as she and neither could get up the nerve to even speak – much less take a walk or go to a community event.

Finally one evening she attended a parlor concert in the home of a friend from school, Miss. Mary Elizabeth Spencer. The pianist was her cousin, Mr. Robert Spencer, who was visiting from West Point where he was in his final year of Military Academy. Edith was mesmerized by his playing, to the point where Mary Elizabeth, seeing her former classmate staring transfixed at her cousin's dark hair and chiseled features, jabbed her with an elbow and leaned over to whisper.

"Cousin Robert is the pride of our family, we thought he would follow his father's footsteps into law. But he is well on his way to becoming a General. And he is not attached to anyone, dear Edith."

Edith immediately reddened and looked at Mary Elizabeth in horror, was her admiration that obvious? Mary Elizabeth smirked playfully and raised her eyebrows letting her know that, yes, she was.

After the concert, Edith busied herself with gathering her few belongings and then making pleasant conversation with the few friends and family members in attendance. The Spencer family was musical and she always appreciated the conversation she could share with them. Before she had the opportunity to sneak out, she felt a slight touch at her elbow, turning around she was pleased to see Mr. Spencer standing next to her. With a courtly bow he introduced himself, explaining that Mary Elizabeth had mentioned Edith also played the piano.

Before Edith had a chance to think, she was happily conversing with him, easily sharing opinions and experiences about not just music, singing, and piano technique, but also about New York, Plainfield and even opinions concerning the recent presidential election. When others began to trickle out of the parlor and toward their homes she excused herself, secretly feeling reluctant to leave such a pleasant conversation. Her heart skipped a beat when he touched her wrist lightly and shyly asked if he could pay her a call?

She smiled, "Yes, you may. I would enjoy continuing our conversation. Maybe we could even play some songs for four hands."

As she rode in her carriage back toward her house she thought about him with a smile, for the first time she understood why her aunt, friends, and the McArthurs encouraged her to find someone special. She looked forward to seeing him again.

The next few months were a whirlwind of excitement as she got to know Robert Spencer. He called two days later and from that moment on they quickly established a mutual understanding of high regard for one another. Though he had to return to school only three days later, they exchanged letters frequently and for the first time since Liza, Edith allowed herself to trust and be open with someone new. By the following winter when Robert could return to Plainfield no one was surprised when he brought his grandmothers diamond solitaire ring and asked for her hand in marriage. Edith was delighted to say yes and a date was set for the next spring.

The violence and political turmoil around them put a damper on their happiness, however, and Edith couldn't help but wish Robert would take less of an interest in the Union cause. Though she supported his beliefs and was proud of him when he spoke out against slavery, she wished he would be more reserved in the company of wealthy gentlemen who felt it was necessary for the economy. She longed for peace and did not like to hear the gentlemen talk of President Lincoln calling for soldiers to enlist. She knew Robert was eager to establish his military career, but she was hopeful the skirmishes beginning to the south would settle down. She was thankful for her sheltered life far from the disputes and when she wrote letters to Liza describing the political strife Liza was even further removed, saying out west they heard very little about the skirmishes. Liza still wondered what it might be like out in the open plains, far from the bustle and uncertainty surrounding her here.

When she broached the subject with Robert he was surprisingly interested, even taking the time to read a few of her novellas about the adventures out west. His interest and support in her dream of traveling west was sweet, though she knew he saw it as a just a dream. She wondered if it was a possibility she actually wanted, when she read Liza's accounts of her new home. Riding on a stern-wheeler over the Columbia River, moving into their newly constructed hotel, called The Saint Louis after their hotel in San Francisco, their fancy dresses and late nights. It was all so different from her quiet life her.

Edith and Robert were married in a quiet ceremony that spring with his small family and a few friends in attendance. They settled into her family home and tried to begin to enjoy the routine of married life, continuing to play piano and enjoy meals together. Sadly for Edith, though, Robert was more and more occupied with his political involvement. After his graduation from the United States Military Academy he was appointed a 2nd Lieutenant of the Mounted Rifles. After two short months, he joined his fellow military men in Virginia for

what he promised to be a brief scuffle with the
Confederates. Robert wrote cheerful letters to Edith
through July recounting their training and positioning for
the battle he was certain the north would win.
Unfortunately, however, the battle turned out to be
much bloodier and more violent than anyone had
anticipated. On July 23 she received a telegram from
the United States Army informing her that her new
husband had died in battle.

Edith was devastated. She spent the next few
months staying busy taking care of the particulars of his
burial and funeral, grieving with his kind family, and
accepting condolences from his many loved ones.

Then she decided she needed a change of scenery.
Robert had been supportive of her dreams of traveling
west, now that he was gone Edith felt it was the best
choice for her. She wrote to Liza asking if she could visit
the following year, but her response was surprising. Her
usual letters, so optimistic and full of descriptions of
beautiful landscapes and gowns, was brief.

Dear Edith

Please do not leave your comfortable life behind to come out here. I know you are grieving and miss your sweet husband, he was a brave soldier. But joining me in this wild country will just add to your misery. I fear the journey is more than you can do - and alone. You will make your life complete there again.

Love always

Liza

Edith was thrown into a state of even further misery at this letter, she didn't understand why her friend would dismiss her plan so readily. For a time, she considered traveling west anyway, or maybe moving to New York to be nearer Robert's elderly mother. But with time her heart began to mend. Diana stayed by her side, more like family than an employee, and she and Sean made sure Edith ate regularly and got outside for regular walks. After a few months, she forgave Liza her unwillingness to have her travel to visit and, with the help of Diana, she began to see the folly in traveling such a great distance simply to try to escape her feelings of grief. But she still consoled herself with books about the wild frontier and Liza's chatty letters, wondering if she would ever be anything other than a retiring society lady.

Chapter Seventeen

The Saint Louis Hotel in Walla Walla

Liza was briefly thrilled when she first received a letter from Edith saying she would like to join her in Walla Walla. To be reunited at last! But when she shared the letter with Josephine and Olympia their eyes widened. Liza's friends knew of Liza's step-sister, knew how Liza had spent one golden year living with the Crawford family in their comfortable mansion in New York, and they knew that Edith was innocent as to the worldly ways of Liza and the rest. Before Liza even had a chance to finish reading, Jo was shaking her head.

"Liza, what would she do here? A woman of breeding and education, here? Where would she stay?" Josephine's face was full of concern for her friend.

Liza furrowed her brow. "Well, here? I had not really considered..." She trailed off, realizing her friend would be shocked and frightened at Liza's daily life.

Though The Saint Louis Hotel, newly constructed and opulent, was the most elegant establishment in the entire region, someone of Edith's station would not readily accept the business negotiations that allowed Liza, Olympia, Honoria and the rest to live so comfortably on the top floors. The idea of Edith, her innocent blue eyes taking in the raucous nightly festivities and playful banter with gentlemen, made Liza shudder.

"And that journey," Olympia added. Like Liza, Olympia had traveled west on a wagon train with her parents and would never forget the physical discomfort and difficulty. Olympia still spoke with a shudder of her father drowning while trying to caulk their wagon across the Colorado River, and having to continue on with her mother and infant brother even though they could never recover his body. She recalled her shoes falling to shreds and having to walk barefoot the last month, arriving in San Francisco with absolutely nothing and then losing both her mother and brother a few months later to illness. Liza had never heard her friend talk of her past before and the brief description she gave was enough, some tragedies are too terrible to contemplate.

With that, Liza wrote to Edith, tears streaming down her face. She longed to see her, longed to revisit her happy childhood. But both Jo and Olympia were right, this was not the right environment for Edith, or for anyone who had a choice. Liza considered her own mother, who rarely wrote and seemed to be slipping so far into a world of laudanum and drink that Liza feared she may have to go and retrieve her and bring her to Walla Walla just to care for her. She had begun corresponding with Madge who assured her Rosie was still taking care of herself, though she was spending more time than usual in bed. With a sigh, Liza dealt with her anxieties in the only way she had ever learned how: by ignoring them.

Evenings at The Saint Louis were when Liza came to life. Other girls were tentative, even after many years working. But Liza enjoyed getting dressed, drinking whiskey, and sitting down to a hand or two of cards. Her cheery voice and quick laugh could be heard throughout the parlor and dining room as she entertained the many visitors to the hotel. The Saint Louis had been wildly popular from the moment it had opened that fall and had quickly become a gathering place for all the gentlemen of the booming town. Walla Walla was not a mining town like Lewiston had been, but it's location perfectly situated it to receive large amounts of gold moving out of the Gold Rush. Local outfitters were making a fortune providing materials for the young men who arrived from all over the country seeking gold. The ladies at The Saint Louis were too. Liza threw herself into her work, refusing to think about Edith and her proposed visit.

When Liza did not receive a response for many months she fretted briefly that Edith would come anyway. Thankfully, eventually Edith replied. It was clear she was hurt but understood Liza was looking out for her and only wanted her to be safe and comfortable. Edith was thankful when they resumed their regular cheerful correspondence.

Chapter Eighteen

The Wedding

Of course, not everyone in Walla Walla was happy with the arrival of Dutch Jo and her girls. While they had been staying with Mr. Willis at The Coast House they had maintained their discretion, only entertaining gentlemen in their rooms with the utmost decorum. Within weeks of arriving Honoria had, to no one's surprise, agreed to marry Mr. John Perkins, the young soldier she had met on the Columbia. The girls all attended their wedding dinner, which they held outdoors to enjoy the beautiful August weather.

In attendance was Amelia, a cousin of John Perkins who had accompanied his parents and sister for the wedding. Amelia was sullen and uncommunicative. Her teeth seemed too big for her mouth and she kept her rubbery lips tightly clamped shut over them, giving her a disapproving expression much too old for her 17 years.

John's sister, Nea Perkins, sat stiffly next to her cousin and both girls seemed immediately suspicious of the ladies from The Saint Louis Hotel.

Emblyn, who had been living with her new husband Mr. James Shaw, in Walla Walla ever since the evening they met on the Columbia River, found herself sitting across from Amelia and Nea. Always friendly, Emblyn smiled at the younger girls and asked how they had enjoyed the journey up the Columbia.

Amelia raised one shoulder and kept her expression vacant saying only, "It was satisfactory." In a bored voice.

Emblyn caught the shared look between Nea and Amelia and heard Nea's sharp exhale of air indicating contempt. No stranger to the wrath of upstanding society ladies in her brief time living in San Francisco, Emblyn was surprised to receive such treatment now. Since arriving in Walla Walla both she and her husband had carefully concealed her working life and had established themselves as hardworking people of the valley. Clearly, these two young ladies did not know her and assumed she deserved to be judged. Smiling and nodding toward them politely she rose from the long bench where dinner would be served, moving toward the clearing under the Poplar trees where most of the guests were congregating.

Liza, Julia, and Olympia were laughing, standing together in a friendly group under the shade of a tree. The happy couple had enlisted the captain of Mr. Perkin's regiment to marry them, the sun was just beginning to set as the bride arrived. Honoria was beautiful in a white brocade gown adorned with pearls and a long veil. Her friends smiled to see her so happy, but were even more pleased to see Mr. Perkins. He was clearly thrilled to be marrying Honoria and they knew the couple would have a happy future.

At the dinner, where Mr. Perkins' fellow soldiers had butchered and slow-cooked a pig along with fresh-picked corn and tomatoes, Emblyn once again had to endure the mistreatment of Nea and Amelia. This time, her husband was sitting on one side of her and Liza and Julia on the other. Even the presence of Mr. Shaw did not stop the cousins from ridiculing not just Emblyn but every girl in Josephine's company.

They were clearly aware of the work the ladies engaged in or had previously engaged in and felt it their duty to condemn them for their choices.

Nea, looking down her rather long nose at Liza and screwing up her mouth, spoke to her cousin. "I must say there certainly are a lot of tasteless styles out here in this back woods place, would you not agree, Amelia."

Amelia had giggled meanly, "I was thinking exactly the same thing. If a lady wants to look respectable she should keep her adornment to a minimum. To be so over-beaded and veiled is crass and tasteless."

Sniffing sourly Nea had leaned closer to her cousin and whispered something the other two couldn't hear. Both laughed behind their hands. Mr. Shaw, completely unaware, asked the two ladies how their journey had gone.

Amelia gave him a sweet, genuine smile, admiring his handsome mustache and strong physique. "It was comfortable and beautiful, thank-you. We enjoyed it very much." She lowered her eyelashes, trying to appear coy.

He nodded, remembering, "Yes, that is where I met my dear Emblyn, on the Columbia River Sternwheeler. We will always remember that special time." He patted her hand and smiled adoringly at his wife.

The cousins stared with identical expressions of scorn. "You are married?" Nea asked, attempting to sound pleasant.

Liza had remained surprisingly quiet. Never known to allow anyone to mistreat her or a friend, Liza looked both girls up and down with a critical eye. "Oh yes, they are married. Are either of you married?"

Both Nea and Ameila reddened. They had not realized Emblyn was married to Mr. Shaw and were not pleased.

Now they turned their scorn on Julia, both focusing their unpleasant gazes on her. Julia squirmed uncomfortably, unable to say anything. Liza would not allow anyone to make her feel low and she especially wouldn't allow anyone to hurt one of her friends. Nor could she resist getting in one last dig:

"You know, if you are looking for work, I heard there is a new brothel opening up in Pendleton. They aren't too selective."

Both ladies drew in their breath sharply, wearing matching expressions of shock. She met their eyes back with a steady strength that soon caused both to look down.

When, a few moments later, Mr. Edward Jennings joined them at the table and greeted Julia in particular, they both looked sharply at Julia's hand to see if she was wearing a ring. It was obvious Amelia was interested in capturing a husband and now she had her sights set on Edward who looked handsome wearing his dapper soldier uniform to see his friend get married.

"Why Julia, don't you look pretty this evening! Hello Emblyn, Liza, what a pleasure." Edward said before turning to the two newcomers with a smile.

Amelia's eyes blazed, shifting them briefly toward Julia, she then turned her charm onto Mr. Jennings. Though she was neither pretty nor particularly kind, she was crafty and she captured his attention by showering him with attention and flattery. Julia and Liza, who had no interest in Mr. Jennings for anything more than an occasional client, watched in amusement. Julia, Liza, and Emblyn soon lost interest in the pitiful intrigue instigated by young Amelia and, after enjoying their meal and a pleasant conversation, they left with Mr. Shaw to visit with their friends and take part in the rest of the wedding festivities.

When Mr. Jennings came to The Saint Louis three months later to celebrate his engagement to Amelia, the irony was not lost on the girls when he asked to end the celebration alone with Julia in her room.

Liza asked him if Miss Amelia might not disapprove and he had looked at the ground briefly, "Well, I wouldn't want her to find out. But she's not the type of girl that would have any way of finding out, so I'm not too worried."

Liza laughed her tinkling laugh, playfully swatting him on the arm. He looked up at her and finally saw the humor in the situation and laughed too.

"I just wanted to please my mother," he offered by way of explanation.

"Well she should be just right tickled pink." Liza called, as Julia led him up the stairs.

Chapter Nineteen

A night at The Saint Louis

Liza pulled her curly blonde hair up onto her head, admiring her reflection at the mirror in the parlor. She noted how the pink of the setting summer sun softened the slight wrinkles forming around the corners of her eyes. Tossing her hair back, she laughed, what did it matter? She was still the most popular girl here, well, maybe woman might be more accurate. But more of the guests requested her than any other girl, despite the fact that she was one of the older girls.

Jo came in, quickly scanning the room to make sure everything was in order before allowing the night's festivities to begin. Clementine was already asleep with Ruby in attendance in her private third floor chambers and Josephine was dressed in a customary modest and elegant gown. Liza tried to keep her face calm and placid so as not to annoy her in any way. Because although

Liza did not mind a good argument, she had learned through their many years of working together that she would never get the best of her employer in an argument when it came to her establishment. Josephine Wolfe insisted on the best, and when she wanted the best, she got it.

From the moment they had arrived in Walla Walla three years earlier, Jo had always taken care of her girls. Liza had shown her a fierce loyalty back in the days as they had traveled together from San Francisco to open the first Bordello in Walla Walla Territory, and she was kind and generous in return. She also would not allow any type of indiscretion. Yes, they may work in a house of ill repute, but they were also the most highly regarded with the most respectable clientele, and Jo would not allow any hint of misbehavior. Not a hint.

This also meant that she often frowned on what Liza considered just plain old-fashioned fun. What was some loud singing or a bawdy dance? What was a shot or two of whisky, if the gentlemen in question didn't take offense? Liza had always been known as the most fun-loving and cheerful of all the girls, and her popularity with all the wealthiest clients showed that her manner of fun was not frowned upon. At least not by anyone but Dutch Jo.

Jo nodded happily at Julia who, because of her natural reserve, was always the perfect example of decorum. Then she turned her penetrating gaze onto Liza, a trace of amusement playing around her face as she looked her old friend up and down to check for inappropriately risqué clothing or a hidden flask of whiskey. Liza knew to keep herself in check, though, and this evening was certainly no different. She smoothed her dress, a lovely silk calico recently arrived on the steamship from Portland. The silk had come clear from far-off China and the seamstress from Portland had made everyone new dresses from similar cloth. The puffed sleeves and fitted waist accentuated her hourglass figure and the hat she was carefully pinning in place was embellished with a large ostrich feather. Jo was clearly pleased and nodded as she looked Liza over. Though Josephine had a lot of responsibility with her new establishment, she still enjoyed light-hearted pursuits such as beautiful gowns or lively conversation.

The Saint Louis Hotel was the most elegant and sophisticated of the five parlor houses located in Walla Walla and many of the finest gentlemen of the community visited the establishment. The mayor, the sheriff, even the physician were known to pay a call. Some of the ladies from the other, smaller, parlor houses had tried to move over to Dutch Jo's, though Jo had only invited one to come work with them. A girl named Daisy who was both pretty and intelligent offered Jo a promise that her experience as a working girl from Portland made her a benefit to the hotel.

Though Daisy was a little over-dramatic, she was a welcome addition since the occasional girl would find herself with child and have to sit in confinement for many months. Most choose to have the baby removed, a dangerous and painful process that ran the risk of illness or worse. A few, including Irma and Olympia had elected to have the babies, though Josephine discouraged this. Irma had found a home for her infant son, but Olympia's small daughter was still living in The Saint Louis, joining Clementine and Ruby on the third floor.

A carriage could be heard pulling in front of The Saint Louis, Jo bustled down the hall to open the door to the first guests of the evening. Three dignified merchants came through the door, smiling as they saw Liza and Julia coming down the stairs to greet them in the parlor.

"Josephine! Elizabeth! What a pleasure it is to see your smiling faces." Mr. Jennings beamed his round face at the ladies. The livery owner was happier than ever to be at The Saint Louis since his marriage to his shrewish wife. Though most of the girls rarely ventured out into the finer society the likes of Mrs. Jennings enjoyed, simply looking out the window on a day when she might be passing nearby (never in front of The Saint Louis, of course, but on the way to the milliner half a block away) it was clear that this sour-faced woman was unkind to her husband.

Mr. Jennings was soon engaged in a lively conversation with Liza as he sipped a strong whiskey from Jo's finest cask. Mr. Jennings was a generous patron and they all enjoyed his company, but it was clear to everyone that his affections were especially reserved for young Julia. Julia, though, being Julia, would not be down for at least another 45 minutes as her toilette was complicated.

He was duly rewarded when the fresh-faced Julia finally made it down the stairs, her new pink silk gown gathered becomingly around her slender hips. Her large dark eyes downcast demurely as she she descended the ornate staircase. Mr. Jennings had been telling Liza about a new shipment of tack that had recently arrived at his livery but when his favorite girl came down he trailed off mid-sentence. Liza gave him a playful little push toward Julia with a smile.

Chapter Twenty

Julia

Julia Fawkes had lived in San Francisco with Josephine and Liza since she was 19. A quiet girl, she rarely spoke to any of her friends about her early life. She had traveled with her parents and four siblings from Missouri when she was a small girl. They had endured the difficult terrain, cold and damp, and endless walking before her father had taken on a sudden fever and died. Her mother had been a stoic and hardworking woman who had quietly resigned herself to her fate, continuing on the journey with Julia and her other children. They had arrived in the Oregon Territory with scarcely more than their clothing, even their shoes had worn through. Julia's two older brothers had heard about the gold being found in San Francisco and had left the rest of the family behind to seek a living. Julia had helped her mother tend to the baby and her younger sister, barely surviving off the small amount her mother made weaving hats.

Julia's mother remarried soon after their arrival, a kind man named Daniel Greer who eked out a living by working from sunup to sundown on their meager farm. By the time Julia was sixteen her mother had four more children. When Julia married Verne Ames, a neighboring farmer, she left one home of endless labor and drudgery for another. Though she quickly learned caring for six younger children was preferable to caring for a quick-tempered man twelve years her senior. Julia knew no other life than that of a suffering daughter then wife, however, and she endured as cheerfully as she could.

But then her husband decided they should rent out their farm and travel to San Francisco and join her older brothers in the gold mines. Julia may have worked too much and her marriage to Verne was lonely, but she did not want to leave her home and family. However, Verne was not a husband who listened to his wife or cared what she wanted and within a few short weeks they were leaving.

The day they had left the farm, their small wagon packed with most of their belongings, her family had turned out to tell her good-bye. Her younger brother Timothy had run behind the wagon, waving and crying her name. Something in her broke that day. She waved back and wondered when she would see them again.

Her husband was a miserable, sallow-faced man who spent most of his time complaining about trifling discomforts. He had courted her only briefly, and had presented her as someone who would give her an easier life, away from the constant hardship and crying babies. Instead he expected her to wait on him, always finding fault with her every move. He spent most of the journey by wagon to the steamship berating her for bringing too many belongings. He was concerned they would not be able to sell any excess items when they sold their wagon and would be forced to leave them behind, something he could not bear to do. When they arrived and were easily able to sell everything, giving them plenty of money for travel and extra left over for their arrival, he didn't even look at her. Instead, he just marched ahead, glaring at any man who even glanced at Julia's luminous white face.

Julia was unaware of her rare beauty. Though she had been told as a young child traveling to Oregon Territory that she was pretty by some of the younger girls traveling, it hadn't really mattered to her. She rarely saw anyone outside of her immediate family and her luxurious chestnut hair and flawless skin did nothing to ease the difficult labor of caring for children and farm work. But as she and her sullen husband boarded the large steamship bound for San Francisco she was surprised by the many male eyes trained on her every move.

She realized there were few women, but even with those that were around, Julia commanded attention that was startling. Her husband did not like it and accused her of flaunting herself in a most un-Christian way. Julia took offense to this.

"Verne, you know I have no intention of attracting the attention of anyone, but especially not from gentlemen." She said in her customary quiet voice. "Please forgive me if you feel I have brought this on myself."

He glowered at her, then shot angry looks at a few of the sailors who were trying not to notice her. "You will stay in our cabin. I don't want you to attract any unwanted advances. You are a good woman."

Julia lowered her head, keeping her eyes trained on the backs of his feet as she followed him into their tiny cabin. She felt a tiny stab of resentment as she saw the ocean spread out before her, it was gray and vast and presented a beauty she had never experienced. She longed to lean over the railing and take it in, especially as the ship was heading out to the open sea.

But instead, she found herself in her windowless cabin, clutching her stomach, fighting off seasickness. Verne stayed above, probably enjoying the view. She spent the first three hours curled up in a ball on her narrow bunk, the rocking of the boat making her feel more and more ill with each passing moment. She longed for some fresh air.

Finally, she could bear it not longer. She flung open the door and dashed up the metal stairs to the open deck, clutching her full skirts. Feeling the salty wind on her face gave her instant relief. She took in great gulping breaths as she leaned against the railing.

"You look a little green." She heard a light, high voice next to her. Even before she turned she imagined it's owner was smiling.

The girl, who was just a few years older than Julia, looked cheerfully at her from beneath an elaborate feathered hat. Her brown hair curled prettily around her face. She wore a yellow gown adorned with pearl buttons and lace. Julia looked down at her own homespun dress and was so curious about this young girl she nearly forgot her stomach pain entirely.

"Don't worry, I rode over with Mr. Foster from San Francisco last week. Just keep your eyes on the horizon and you'll soon feel just fine." Sally told her.

Julia had so many questions she didn't know where to begin. Why had she travelled just the week before? How could her dress be so beautiful? Who was Mr. Foster? But before she had a chance to ask any questions Verne arrived.

He was livid. His usually pale face was red with anger. "How dare you emerge from your room?" He hissed at Julia. "What kind of woman do you want people to mistake you for?"

He glared at the girl in yellow who returned his stare with a calm smile. She appeared completely unconcerned by his rude intimation.

As he was forcefully pulling Julia back toward the stairs, she leaned over and whispered, "I can help you."

Julia looked back at her as a distinguished-looking gentleman in a top hat joined her at the railing. She heard the girl laugh a light tinkling laugh as her husband berated her for being out of her room.

Julia endured his wrath, barely explaining her illness and need for fresh air. She knew her best option was to simply look passively at the ground and that he would soon tire of screaming at her. Eventually he left her alone again, reminding her gruffly to remain in the room. When, a few minutes later she heard a light tap at the door she wondered if he had returned, though he would never be so polite as to knock before entering.

Opening the door tentatively, she was surprised to see the young lady once again. She was wearing a broad smile as she stood out in the dark hall.

"I could hear your husband hollering at you from the very top of the stairs. That's quite the master you've got there." She said with a forward confidence Julia would have found shocking if it hadn't been such an honest assessment.

She was unsure of what to do. She opened the door a little wider and stammered out, "Wo-Woul you like to come in?"

The lady shook her head. "No thank you. I wouldn't want to be caught here by your husband. If I see any feet descending the stairs I will just go right around the corner and you will just shut your door and I pray say nothing about me. Mr. Foster would not be happy if your husband screamed at me that way."

"Who is Mr. Foster?" Julia asked. She could have asked a hundred questions, but this seemed like an easy one to start with.

The girl laughed her tinkling laugh. "Well, for this month he's my employer. I like to think I'm his favorite."

Julia was confused. "Your employer? What do you do?"

"Well, I don't do hard labor. I don't work outdoors. And I certainly don't get yelled at or locked in my room." She said, adjusting her large silk hat.

Julia narrowed her eyes. "Do you mean, you are a fallen woman?"

The girl laughed. "I suppose I am. I don't know how far I've fallen, though, considering I am enjoying life quite a bit." She stopped laughing, her face suddenly serious. "But I suspect your life isn't all that much fun. In fact, when I saw the way your husband treats you I saw a little of my own sad past in your eyes."

Julia felt conflicting emotions rising up inside her. The girl was right, she was unhappy, but what did that matter? As a woman, it wasn't her place to be happy. Right?

As if sensing what she was feeling, the girl reached across the threshold of the cabin door and patted her hand gently. "Forgive me for barging in like this." She said, no longer flippant or even cheerful. Her brown eyes looked deeply into Julia's, showing only concern. Julia felt her judgement against the girl softening.

"Let me introduce myself," the girl continued. "I am Sally Ketchum, from San Francisco. I couldn't help noticing how sad you looked and I was hoping I could help. You reminded me of myself, before I took the reins on my own life."

Julia felt a little more confident in the presence of this exotic girl. Until this point, Julia had only known hard work and loss. This girl seemed to come from a different life and she found herself intrigued.

"Where do you live?" She asked.

Sally was pleased to tell her the name. "The Saint Louis Hotel, in San Francisco." She barely had time to give some brief directions before they heard heavy footsteps coming down the narrow stairs. Both women immediately bolted, Sally was safely around the corner as Verne threw the door open. He showed no pleasure in seeing his wife, quietly crocheting, only nodding solemnly as he walked in.

Each day of the three day journey Sally visited Julia, knocking softly on her door just moments after Verne left to take in the fresh sea air on the upper decks. Sally was glad to have another young woman to visit with on the boat, even if it was for only a brief moment, and she was eager to describe the beauty and excitement of San Francisco.

On the third day, as Julia was preparing their trunk for their arrival, Sally arrived for their now-customary morning conversation. Julia opened the door and smiled at her new friend, admiring her ruffled pink dress adorned with lace and beadwork.

"I brought you something." Sally said, holding out a pair of beautiful mother-of-pearl combs.

Julia stared at the lovely combs, unable to reach for them.

"They are too lovely! I could never..." She started to say.

Sally just smiled more widely and pushed them toward her. "Please, take them. They suit your coloring better than mine. They were a gift from another gentleman and he will never know."

Julia tentatively took them, admiring their delicate beauty. She clutched them to her heart and looked at Sally. "How can I repay you? You have been so kind to me."

Sally just laughed. " All those stuffy ladies up there in first class, eating in the fancy dining hall - I don't want to talk to them. You need a friend! When I saw you I remembered what it was like to not have my own life, to have an unhappy man control my every move." Her cheery face clouded for a moment as she remembered. She leaned closer and whispered, "Remember, The Saint Louis Hotel, in San Francisco. If things get to be too much for you, I'll make sure you're welcome with us. Life doesn't have to be like this."

And with that, Sally turned and swished back down the hall, her jaunty walk and elaborate hat a shock of bright color in the dull gray corridor.

When Julia and Verne arrived in San Francisco they fought the crowds to rent a carriage to carry them to the small apartment her brothers were renting on Pacific Street. Both Edmund and Reginald had been living in a nearby mining camp until recently. Though the number of gold seekers arriving daily gave them new opportunities. They had recently opened a small mining outfitter and were living in the small apartment above the storefront. As housing was scarce, they had agreed to allow Verne and Julia to stay with them provided Julia did the cooking and helped run the shop.

Julia soon realized she would be working in conditions even more deplorable than the terrible drudgery of her past. She now lived in a tiny one room apartment with three men, filthy from frequent trips to nearby mining camps. She was expected to rise before dawn each day, wash their clothing and get it hung out to dry on the roof, cut wood and build a fire so she could make coffee and breakfast, then run the mining shop. The neighborhood they were living in was crowded and noisy and full of the worst vice. Crass and belligerent gentlemen stomped in all day, demanding service and sometimes hinting that she would provide services she had no intention of giving. The few women she saw were scantily clad and usually stumbling drunk, though most women stayed inside the cheap saloons and brothels lining the streets. Music and yelling could be heard at all hours of the day and night.

Verne began spending more and more time away from her, though she did not mind, because when he was with her he was so sullen and withdrawn she felt she was tiptoeing on glass. Her brothers, too, seemed to enjoy the chaos and excitement of the environment and spent their time either at the mining camps, stocking their provisions, or at one of the nearby saloons. Julia was surprised, though not entirely. After her father's death, her brothers had always been allowed to run wild.

She went about her chores methodically, willing herself not to think, trying to think of a better life. Her mind continuously returned to Sally, the young girl from the boat. She wondered if The Saint Louis Hotel was loud and dirty like the neighborhood she had found herself in. She highly doubted it.

One morning, about a month after she had arrived, she moved about the dark apartment shivering. She had slept poorly as usual, she only had one thin blanket and was sleeping on the floor. Though she had attempted to explain to Verne and her brothers, they had silenced her immediately and she had no way to procure another blanket or any bedding. The three men were snoring comfortably, snugly covered with warm blankets, and she prepared breakfast. The afternoon before, she had sold her beautiful mother-of-pearl combs, the gift from Sally, so she could buy a small amount of food for the household.

Though she was certain they were all making good money; she saw how much went into the cash register from the outfitting and she knew how much gold was being brought into the city, somehow food was scarce. Reginald kept meticulous records of the books and counted the money every day. He would not allow her to even touch the money once it had entered the register. It seemed they were spending the majority of their money at the neighboring houses of pleasure. When she had asked Verne for money the day before he had cuffed her across the cheek and told her to go out and earn some money if she felt she was so poorly off.

"What?" He had yelled, his eyes a strange glassy red, "Do you think I just need to give you everything so you can sit around here all day?" Then he had left, banging the door shut behind him.

She had felt tears welling up in her eyes but had turned quickly away, she would not give him the pleasure of seeing her cry.

The morning before, she had only been able to find some stale bread, and not nearly enough for the three of them. As she had stood looking in the empty cupboard, wondering what to do, as she remembered her combs. She could sell her combs. It hadn't been difficult, she had simply stood in front of the shop and stopped a bright-eyed young man about to enter one of the parlor houses. He had been happy to give her some of his newly acquired gold dust in exchange for the combs.

And now she was able to prepare breakfast. For today. But she had nothing more to sell, and she needed to address the issue of money with her husband and brothers. As they sat down she waited for them to finish their eggs before speaking up.

"I managed to procure a little food for us, but I will need a little money for the household." She said, hoping she would not anger anyone.

Her husband instantly banged his fist onto the table, the plates jumped, clanging onto the tabletop.

"Woman! Did I not tell you, go out and earn some money! Sew hats! Sell flowers! There is plenty of gold to be found around here, you don't need to be asking us to help you."

Her brothers just sat, chewing, staring into space. She wondered if they even heard. All any of them seemed to care about was work and then going out to visit the saloons, they were suddenly like strangers to her.

She looked at the floor, silent. Something inside her snapped at that moment. Where normally she might have felt apologetic for even asking, suddenly she felt angry. Why were they treating her like this? She had never wanted to leave her family and come up here! Verne had dragged her to this lawless city full of too much gold and too much vice and somehow he had gotten sucked in and had abandoned her. He had never been much of a husband to her, but now he was treating her worse than a dog.

As she stood there, waiting for them to finish their breakfasts so she could eat her own meager residuals and then clean up, she fumed silently, plotting. She would not take this treatment even one more day. She had an escape and she was going to use it.

By that afternoon she was standing in front of the elegant doorway of The Saint Louis Hotel. Far from the bustle and vagaries of her brief previous residence, The Saint Louis provided an immediate respite as she stepped inside the hushed lobby. She looked down at her drab cotton dress and flushed at how she must look in a fancy place like this. She prayed Sally was here and that she would remember her.

She heard the swish of a skirt behind her and an elegantly dressed older woman appeared, she had bright red hair and wore a curious expression.

"I am looking for Sally?" Julia practically whispered.

The woman didn't seem particularly surprised, she simply called up the nearby staircase and a few minutes later Sally peered down from the landing. When she spotted Julia she smiled her bright smile and came down, gathering full skirts around her.

"You gave up on that ol' codger after all!" She said by way of greeting. "I knew you were a strong woman under all that subservience."

Mustering her first smile since she had arrived in San Francisco, Julia nodded proudly. She felt a great burden released now that she was away from the oppression of her husband.

Chapter Twenty-One

Julia's fireman

Julia loved Walla Walla. Though she had enjoyed her years in San Francisco, when Dutch Jo had come back to The Saint Louis and asked some of the girls to accompany her to Oregon Territory Julia had jumped at the chance. She missed her family near Portland, though she had grown accustomed to a life of freedom of comfort and had no desire to return to a life of farm labor. She wrote to her mother and younger siblings, telling them vaguely about her life, omitting large chunks of information, and hoping they wouldn't worry too much about her choices.

She wasn't surprised when her mother wrote angrily to her about the shame of leaving her husband. Her mother urged her to return, certain he would accept her apologies and she would not be seen to poorly in the eyes of the Lord. But Julia simply ignored the subject entirely, instead focusing her written accounts on the weather, the architecture, and gentle daily adventures. Her mother ignored most of her letters, but occasionally sent a letter at Christmas or to let her know about family events.

But San Francisco, for all it's adventure and excitement and wealth, was never the city for Julia. Julia longed for the open sky and rolling hills of the land to the north and she was eager to set out for a new adventure. She longed to start fresh and put even more distance between herself and Verne. Because though she was careful to never reveal to her mother where she lived, always receiving mail through the post office, she still lived in fear that some day Verne would find her and drag her back into his oppressive servitude.

Once established at their own Saint Louis Hotel in Walla Walla, Julia opened up and relaxed. Sally had been right, her life now was so much more enjoyable now that she held her own reins. Living in a beautiful hotel, in her own room, surrounded by friends Julia was finally living a life that gave her reason to smile. She slowly learned to trust men, though at first she had been wary. But with the help friends like Sally and Olympia, she had grown accustomed to fulfilling their needs and soon found it was not so difficult as long as she paid attention and listened to them.

After a few months in The Saint Louis there was great excitement among all the girls because they realized what was being built directly behind their building: a new fire station! Though not many of the volunteer firemen would be there full time, the ladies were happy to know the station would be so close.

Fire fighters were some of the few men who the ladies considered friends, rather than customers. Most were in Walla Walla because of the gold rush in Idaho and spent the winter in the more peaceful and mild Walla Walla. Winters were never particularly pleasant making mining impossible, so the men would stop into Walla Walla until Spring before continuing on to Lewiston.

Fire was a constant fear, the wooden structures, wooden sidewalks, and use of candles and wood fires meant people had to be vigilant to keep fires contained. In the winter, when days were short and cold, fires often sprang up and the people of Walla Walla were grateful for fire clubs downtown. For the small town 60 volunteer firemen was barely enough considering the main means of fighting a fire was the bucket brigade. In the summertime, when the majority of the volunteers left for the mining camps, the fires were less frequent but more likely to burn the buildings to the ground.

When the Union Hook and Ladder Company was formed, their motto "We destroy to save!" was on everyone's lips as they gathered at Dutch Jo's to celebrate their first night. The city didn't pay any of the men, though they were happy to be part of the team. The bright red jackets and smart black caps made the dapper young gentlemen appear official and many of the ladies were smitten. The city had provided the volunteers with uniforms and were also organizing a tournament of physical feats against the Portland and Dalles fire companies.

Julia had noticed a young, black-haired gentleman laughing cheerfully along with the rest of the firefighters. He seemed to be noticing her too, he often looked over at her and smiled. As the evening wore on he came to talk to her and introduced himself as Carl Bellman. He had recently arrived from Portland where he had volunteered.

He chuckled, "We were the Multnomah #1, and our motto was 'Conquer we Must!'"

Julia laughed her gentle laugh. She liked how he seemed good natured and pleasant. She asked about his travels and how he found Walla Walla and was pleased with his cheerful conversation and kindness. Before she knew it, the evening had passed and the remaining firemen were heading back to the station to check on the horses.

Carl was suddenly shy, he bit his lip and asked if she might like to go on a walk some time. She smiled and agreed, eager to know more about this young man.

The firemen often dropped in to visit with the young ladies, though Josephine discouraged them from forming too intimate of a connection. Unlike the wealthier gentlemen of the community, the firemen couldn't afford to pay for the services of the girls. Because of their circumstances and social standing, the upstanding citizens of the town would walk far out of their way to avoid crossing in front of either the fire station or Dutch Jo's establishment. The highly-regarded wives and businessmen of the town didn't want to be seen mixing with anyone of a lower social standing.

For this reason, even though Julia and Carl soon grew closer and desired more of a connection, neither could see how they could breech the great social divide that would have allowed them to live together peacefully. Instead they found solace in their regular walks along Mill Creek and their frequent evening visits on the rooftop balconies.

Chapter Twenty-Two

Rosie

Liza had sent three letters to Rosie and had not received a response. Though she was used to her mother's unreliable behavior, three letters over as many months was too worrisome not to investigate. Liza contacted Marge, who had retired and was still living in a small apartment near The Saint Louis in San Francisco. Marge responded by the next post, letting Liza know she was worried about Rosie. Eva, the current madame in charge of the ladies at The Saint Louis, had argued with Rosie earlier that summer and Rosie had stormed off. Usually when this happened Rosie would eventually return, but this time no one had heard from her. They had given up looking for her and boxed up her possessions.

Liza was thrown into a turmoil. Though Rosie had given her a difficult childhood and had not been able to provide her with the support and stability she would have liked, she was still her mother and Liza needed to help her. With the help of Josephine, she began sending letters to everyone they still knew in San Francisco. Within three weeks they had a response. Rosie was living in a lean-to by the wharf, barely leaving her bed, completely given over to laudanum. She was still working, but in such conditions that even sailors fresh from sea wouldn't normally touch her. The lady who wrote was an older woman named Cora who had worked at The Saint Louis before marrying and becoming the respectable wife of a saloon owner Cora said Rosie had been quite disoriented the previous week when Cora and other ladies from the mission had delivered meals. She promised to check in with her and send another letter as soon as she saw her.

Liza barely finished reading the letter before she was packing a small trunk to make the journey back. Josephine knew there would be no way to stop her, so she gave her some extra cash and wished her well. Liza barely noticed the steamboat up the river, she didn't even have a chance to be grateful for the smooth sailing up the river or the even smoother transit from Portland to San Francisco on the larger Steamer. By the time Liza arrived to San Francisco she was nearly frantic with worry. She rented a carriage and raced down to the wharf where she spent a terrible hour peeking into lean-to structures and tents, calling her mother's name. She was soon faced with the grim sight of a run down, alleyway lined with toothless and grim ladies standing or sitting idly in front of pieces of boards strung together for the most minor shelter. A few toothless, most filthy, the former good-time girls had now disintegrated into the lowest form of working lady. Liza knew she would find her mother here and when she saw her, sitting in a pile of rags, staring despondently at the ground in front of her, she knelt before her.

"Mother?" She said in a whisper, trying to get Rosie to lift her head.

Rosie looked at her with dull eyes. She showed no recognition. Though it had only been three years since they had last seen each other, Rosie appeared to have aged decades.

"Rosie?" Liza tried again, this time in a stronger voice.

Hearing her own name, Rosie's eyes flashed in recognition. She appeared to be lost in a world of opiates, an empty laudanum

bottle lay on it's side nearby. She looked at Liza and smiled, showing blackened teeth.

"My girl." She croaked, her eyes shining with life briefly before snuffing out just as quickly.

Liza tried to pull her to her feet, but she wouldn't budge. "Mother, I can take you to a better place than this. I can bring you home with me. We will support you, you don't have to live like this." She said, her voice growing frantic.

But Rosie just shook her head. "Go away, I'm working." She said impatiently. A man was shuffling up the street. Rosie attempted a smile, but he looked at Liza, his grizzled face hopeful.

Liza was appalled. She shook her head briskly and stood up. "Mother!" She was now angry, was Rosie's headache medicine more important than her dignity?

More important than her life? "Please stand up and come with me!"

But Rosie would not budge. Rosie contemplated dragging her out, screaming at her, hiring the carriage to come get her...but she realized she could not do any of these things. Instead she decided to try again the next morning, hoping maybe her mother would be more clear-headed at that point.

But the next morning, after checking out of the inn and taking another carriage to her mother's dilapidated home, she was greeted with an even more stubborn negativity. This time Rosie was more clear-headed, but she needed her laudanum and she was anxious for Liza to help her get more. Quickly.

When Liza refused Rosie yelled, "Then leave me alone if you aren't going to help me!"

Liza backed away, temporarily embarrassed by the scene, then realizing none of the other ladies nearby were any better off and nobody cared. Liza was nearly fed up. She told her mother she would not help her destroy herself and she would be back the next day.

Liza gave it one more chance, arriving early the next morning. This time Rosie didn't even get out of her bed. Liza poked her head into the dirty and pungent room, covering her nose with her hand to keep out the smell. Rosie lay staring blissfully up at the boards and blankets above her head.

"I'm here mother." Rosie spoke softly, unsure how her mother would respond. "The carriage is just a short walk, please get your things and we'll go get on the ship."

But Rosie did nothing more than just flick her eyes toward her daughter and shake her head slowly.

Liza felt the tears sliding down her cheeks as she backed back out into the fresh air of the alley way. She had done all she could. She softly said good-bye, though she knew her mother couldn't hear her, then she returned to the ship yard to book passage back to Walla Walla.

Chapter Twenty-Three

Liza's Grief

Liza started drinking whiskey heavily after she returned from San Francisco. Whiskey, delivered weekly on the boats from Lewiston, had become her solace. For a while, she had just listlessly stared into space, unable to enjoy life. But that was before. After a few seasons she woke up and realized there was still fun to be had and Liza's biggest challenge was usually finding someone to share the fun with her. On occasion a gentleman would come into The Saint Louis who had the same joy for staying up late, telling stories and drinking whisky as Liza and everyone would think she might finally settle down, maybe even get married and leave the working girl life. But eventually something had always happened. The first, almost two years ago, had been a buffalo hunter who had disappeared from one week to the next. Everyone assumed he must have been killed in his dangerous profession. Liza refused to talk about him.

The second time, he had been a young man, a merchant three years her junior. The other girls giggled amongst themselves that Liza must have been his first experience with a woman because Luther had been so entranced with her. Olympia started calling him her puppy and Daisy teased that she wanted to be a bridesmaid at their wedding. Liza had been so cheerful at this time, a more focused healthy cheer than her usual never-ending good-time girl ways. She started getting up earlier, helping out around the hotel with decorating and helping younger girls, lending a hand with the cooking. When Luther would come to the hotel she was calmer and drank much less than usual.

After a few months, it began to seem Luther really might be that special someone who would turn Liza's life around. She had never harbored hope of living a "respectable" life like some of the other girls. Her mother had worked her entire life until falling ill and dying and Liza had always expected she would have to do the same. But for the first time, she was beginning to see a glimmer of hope and she was so eager for the possibility she could barely speak of it.

When Luther would come to the hotel he would often sit in the parlor and discuss the sale of feed and livestock with other merchants from town. He was young and eager to please the older gentlemen who came to the establishment and would sit for many hours strategizing ways to increase the sales of his products. But one evening Liza came down the stairs slightly later than usual. He had not come the evening before and the previous evening he had seemed distant so she had asked Julia to try a special hairstyle, hoping to please him. However, when she arrived in the parlor Liza was surprised to see Luther speaking not to the other merchants from town but instead to Daisy, the new girl who had recently come to work for Jo from the The Good Time Saloon.

Liza felt a brief flash of worry. Daisy was much younger than Liza, though still not as pretty with her thin face and spotted, uneven skin. But she had a charm and flattery about her that men seemed to like and she seemed to be using it in full force on Luther. But when

Liza swept over and sat next to Luther, Daisy looked up with a big smile.

"Liza! We were just talking about how much fun you are! I was telling Luther you have the most songs in your repertoire of any of us. See if Francis will play so you can sing something."

Liza wasn't going to be fooled by this girl. She had seen how Daisy had been looking at Luther and she didn't buy for a moment Daisy didn't have an ulterior motive. Ignoring Daisy, Liza turned to Luther and gestured coyly toward the stairs. She was just about to stand up when he surprised her by turning back toward Daisy and asking her if she could sing.

Daisy giggled and looked down at the floor, "I'm shy about it. I only sing if there isn't an audience." She coyly looked up through her eyelashes at the baby faced man, licking her lips suggestively. "But maybe if we were...alone?"

Liza wasn't about to let this fake trollop take her best client. Leaning forward, she allowed her ample cleavage to spill toward the young man.

"Luther, I have something I've been saving for you."
She murmured in his ear.

But Luther was gazing at Daisy, who had now put her finger in her mouth and cocked her head to the side. Liza, realizing this new girl who had previously been friendly toward her, was now blatantly stealing her man, she watched helplessly as the two walked upstairs together. Daisy's loud giggling could be heard even once they were out of sight.

Though Liza pretended not to notice, she drank much more whisky in the months following Luther's betrayal than she ever had before, ending up drinking herself sick when, six weeks later, Daisy skipped out of The Coast House arm in arm with Luther, to be married.

The third time she had a special client she had been less open, he was older and they had shared a calmer regard. Fred Patterson, a charming southerner just arrived from Portland, had been quite taken with Liza, coming to see her at least four nights a week, bringing her flowers and candy. At first she had been thrilled with him, telling all the girls how funny and sweet he was. But as time wore on she started getting less cheerful about his visits, claiming he had difficulty in his work and she was trying to help him through it. After a few months his visits became stressful to everyone at The Coast House. He would enter the parlor, immediately pull Liza up to her boudoir and the shouting would commence. Dutch Jo would put on her most stoic expression and march up after them to end the argument, leaving Liza angry at Jo for kicking him out.

At this time there was a lot of tension at the hotel, for many girls it looked like Liza and Jo might have to part ways. Though Dutch Jo was unendingly polite and kept her temper in check even through the most vicious screaming attacks from Liza, it was clear the proprietress was not going to allow any patron to abuse one of her girls. Even if the girl thought she was in love. It came to the point the evening after a particularly loud argument when the man arrived at the door and Jo would not allow him to enter.

"You are not welcome here." Jo said sternly as she stood, straight-backed at the entrance of the hotel.

Patterson rolled his eyes, his gray face full of contempt as he tried to push past Jo. She held up her arm and stepped toward him.

"You will leave sir, and you will not return. This is a dignified establishment and we will not tolerate abuse."

Patterson hollered up the stairs, "I am here for you Baby! Come on down, I love you and I will give you the life you deserve. These ladies don't care about you."

Just as Jo was shutting the door there was a clattering behind her. Liza was coming down the stairs, her face streaked with tears. She was pulling on her wool jacket and carried her small battered suitcase. Without giving the rest of the girls a glance she pushed past her close friend and went out the door with Fred.

Jo closed the door, her head held high, her face as void of expression as always. But the girls couldn't help but notice the shaking of her chin as she fought back tears before she quickly walked upstairs to her own chamber for the remainder of the evening.

For three months Jo did not speak of Liza's sudden departure. The girls tried to soothe the blow of her friend's sudden disappearance by baking delicious cakes and bringing her tea, but nothing would make her smile during this time. She paid frequent calls to Sheriff Gilliam and even began having long discussions with known members of the town Vigilante committee. One, a gruff man named Marcus Donnehue, began to visit The Coast House almost nightly. Though he never ventured upstairs, he and Josephine could be seen speaking at a small table until late into the night, sometimes joined by other members of the the Vigilantes.

It did not take the ladies long to discover what Jo was up to: she was looking for Liza. Fred Patterson was a suspicious and shifty character and Jo did not think Liza would be safe with him, her evening discussions with Donehue, Sheriff Gilliam and the others others was more than just a friendly visit. Jo knew the men had a finger on the pulse of the valley and she was doing her best to stay informed of her good friend. The men of Walla Walla had their own interest in Patterson and they were working with Josephine to find him.

One spring morning, three months after Patterson had taken Liza away, Jo returned from her regular trip to the greengrocer walking with even more determination than usual. Not even removing her wool coat upon entering the hotel, she called up the stairs for Sally before continuing through to the back where Francis stayed in his small room. Without giving much more of an explanation than that they needed to hurry, she bundled Sally and Francis up with her and jumped into Mr. Donnehue's carriage just as he and Sheriff Gilliam pulled out in front of The Coast House.

The rest of the girls, all in various stages of just waking up for the day, peered out doorways and windows and looked at each other in worry. What was their mistress up to?

The next evening they found out. Just as the first girls were coming downstairs in their pretty dresses, prepared for an evening of pleasantry with their gentlemen callers, the carriage pulled back in front of the hotel. But this time they had someone else with them. The figure was barely able to walk on her own, Jo and Francis supported her on each side, and it took the girls a few minutes to realize they were looking at their friend Liza.

Everyone rushed to open the door, get her inside and upstairs, and try to help her. Jo pushed everyone away and she and Sally carried Liza up to Jo's own chamber, shutting the door. Sheriff Gilliam doffed his hat with courtesy before driving off with Mr. Donnehue and Francis just walked by without meeting anyones gaze, shaking his head.

"Just make good decisions, Ladies." Was all he mumbled as he shuffled toward his room.

It took some time to get the story out of Sally; Jo said absolutely nothing and Francis would only shake his head and remind the girls that there were better ways to make money. But eventually it became clear what had happened.

Fred Patterson had taken Liza to a mining camp where she had settled in to be his mistress. They were living in a tiny tin shanty on the edge of the muddy mountain area, surrounded by identical little huts. But of course it hadn't lasted long before Patterson began to mistreat her and before long he had abandoned her there. But Sally gave a chilling description of Liza's circumstances when they arrived.

"There were men lined up outside her little shack, just waiting their turn to be with her. I swear, they didn't even remove their boots or their hat, and I counted 22 men just there waiting for their poke at her. It was terrible." Sally, who had been a working girl longer than any of them, was ghostly white as she recounted the filthy men, stopping by for a quick visit with a listless and immobile Liza after working all day in the silver mines.

Liza, had even less to say. She came down to the parlor the next night, dressed in a modest cotton dress, though she didn't speak to anyone for a week. She sat in the rocking chair by the corner, an old gray blanket tucked around her shoulders, looking much older and sadder than before her ordeal. She didn't seem to hear any of the lively chatter surrounding her, nor did she focus her gaze on anyone, she just sat rocking and staring off into space. But she was with everyone else, she was alive, and she seemed to perk up whenever Francis would play the piano.

Everyone was relieved when she revealed she still had her strong voice and quick temper a week later. She was in her now customary position near the fire, not appearing to hear anything going on around her. Olympia was arguing in her dignified way with Irma about The Good Time Saloon, the bordello down the street.

"No, Irma," Olympia was saying patiently, "they didn't get here until at least a year after us. Maybe even two."

"Oly, they were here when you all arrived with Miss. Josephine!" Irma proclaimed, her freckled face wrinkled in concentration. I remember that Daisy girl - remember that sneaky girl? I remember her saying they were the first establishment in town."

Liza spoke up from her spot a few feet away, "Irma you are wrong. Those awful Saloon girls are all sneaky liars, especially that Daisy! They didn't open up until two years ago, and they never have been as nice, either!"

Everyone fell quiet after this short speech, they were so surprised to hear Liza say something. Olympia was the first to recover, smiling over at Liza.

"Thanks, Li, I thought I remembered something like that."

Though she occasionally spoke up Liza still carried a sadness around with her and was now subdued and serious. She began to drink more whisky and spent a lot more time sitting near Francis, listening to him play the piano. She never did speak about her ordeal and no one ever asked her to, but if any other girl started to be mistreated by a man or if there was even a hint of impropriety, Liza was now the first to jump up and put a stop to it. Josephine was worried about her friend. She knew Liza had suffered some serious mistreatment on top of the recent loss of her mother and Jo wondered if maybe it might be time for her to retire. She finally devised a plan and when she presented her idea to Liza a spark entered her eyes that Josephine hadn't seen in a long time.

Chapter Twenty-Four

Edith Travels West

Edith had not received a reply from Liza in months, she did not understand what had happened but she was beginning to worry. Liza's letters the previous winter had been full of praise for a man named Fred Patterson, she was clearly smitten with the man. She mentioned he was a southerner who championed the Confederate cause. Though Liza had never before shown any interest in the political dealings of gentlemen, this one statement, mixed in with other flowering praise for her new beau, alarmed Edith. But when she responded and gently asked about his past possible experience with the Confederate army she hadn't received a reply. Could she have angered her friend?

Liza had only written about one other gentleman, Luther, and Edith's heart had ached for Liza when she had later written with a brief description of his betrayal.

Now that she had written about this Fred Patterson, Edith supposed it was quite possible they were now married. She hoped she would hear from Liza soon, and she vowed that she would learn to accept Liza's new husband, Southerner or not. Edith was happy to think of her friend with someone special, she had wondered why Liza never married. She had supposed that with all that gold money she must be doing well and hadn't needed to. Besides helping her friend Josephine run a hotel must take a lot of work, maybe she had simply never had time for gentlemen before.

Edith was beginning to come out of the fog of grief over the loss of Robert and, with the encouragement of the McArthurs she had begun teaching small children piano. Though she did not need the income, the daily interaction with cheerful children was soothing and was helping her join the world again.

One morning that spring, Edith was teaching a small boy named Noah Parsons to play the scales. Noah was musical but not particularly enthusiastic about taking piano lessons, but his mother, a constantly fretting society woman, insisted he join his older sister for twice weekly lessons. Edith choose to meet with Noah first, the half hour consisted mainly of keeping the five year old on the bench and it was exhausting. His older sister sat properly in the parlor with her governess, reviewing her music from the previous lesson, and was an easy break after the lively boy.

Noah picked out a jaunty tune while wiggling his shoulders, a comical show that Edith tried to ignore. Edith tried to keep her face stern. The moment she revealed any mirth the lesson would be lost; the boy lived to make her laugh. Her good humor was cut short, however, by the sudden bustling entrance of Diana McArthur.

"Please forgive the interruption." Diana spoke in a whisper. "But there is a telegraph at the door, and they say it is urgent. They will only give it to you."

Leaving the sparkling-eyed boy with Diana, Edith quickly retrieved the telegraph.

Send the following message to: Edith Crawford

Liza needs you, though she is well. If you are still interested in coming to Walla Walla, we welcome you with and we will arrange a home for you to stay in.

Josephine Wolfe

Edith read it and reread it, struck with a sudden urgency to leave that very day. But the jaunty little tune had turned into the banging of many keys and she needed to take care of her responsibilities here first. She could barely keep her mind on her final two lessons, her head was already out west. What could have happened to Liza? Was she ok? Edith bustled her small charges out the door and immediately began preparations.

The arrangements to head west were complex but her wealth and connections allowed her to find a family connected to her own leaving from Independence the following month. She understood her status as a single woman would be seen as a detriment and that the west was rough and tumble and at times lawless. The vigilante groups could only be counted on to help in established settlements, but on the trail there would be many occasions where a lady like Edith might need more than her polite manners and kind words. It was for this reason that she asked Diana and Sean McArthur to accompany her. Thankfully, they welcomed the opportunity to travel west, something they both saw as not just an adventure, but as a chance for a better life. By the following month, just one year after the loss of her dear husband, they were on their way west.

Once they arrived in Missouri Edith met with the Clarke family with whom she would be traveling. The Clarkes came from a wealthy family in New York and Mr. George Clarke had worked with her father. His sons, Edwin and Terrance, were eager to try their hand as a cattle ranchers in the new Oregon Territory. Their young wives, Myrna and Duncana were sitting in a pretty covered carriage, looking out the window at the hands who were busily carrying supplies. Myrna immediately waved a friendly gloved hand at Edith.

"I do hope you will join us in our carriage." She said with a smile. Though not conventionally pretty, Myrna had a strong confidence and quick smile that instantly put Edith at ease.

Edith obliged, checking to make sure her recently purchased wagon was still being loaded as she sat across from the young ladies.

Duncana, who was a few years older and equally welcoming, patted the velvet cushion she shared with her sister-in-law. "It's a spring-loaded carriage. My cousins traveled over two years ago and are settling in quite comfortably in the Willamette Valley. But they warned us to make sure to ride in a spring loaded carriage, those wagons the others have to sit in can't be too comfortable."

Both ladies shook their heads at the appalling prospect of any discomfort while emigrating on the Oregon Trail. Edith smiled, she was grateful for their planning. Though she had been reading about the journey for years, she hadn't considered what it would be like to travel for months on a bumpy trail.

"Is the other woman your mother?" Duncana asked, gesturing out the small window to where Diana was helping Sean arrange a trunk in the wagon.

"She is like a mother," Edith said, sealing the fate of Diana. From that moment on the McArthurs were more like family than ever. She never revealed to anyone that they had been her servants her entire life and that she was paying them to accompany her. Diana joined them in the carriage and was able to enjoy much of the journey across the country.

Edith could not help but notice the great difference between their group and the majority of the people leaving from Independence. The Clarkes had seven wagons, three-hundred head of cattle, and one-hundred horses with thirty work-hands. The two hands hired to cook had their own wagon and made sure everyone was fed well.

Edith was proud of her own large covered wagon and two oxen as well as three horses and all the tack, supplies, and sundries they would need for a six month journey. Though the outfitters promised there were plenty of places to stop for water and supplies along the way, Edith wasn't taking the risk of running out of anything. Edith was mighty thankful she could afford to pay to accompany such a well-outfitted group as well as her ability to outfit her wagons to capacity. Their group was led by a man called Casper. Casper was a professional Wagon Master and had successfully led many groups along the Oregon Trail, which helped to assuage Edith's mounting apprehension about her journey. She didn't ride in the slow-moving carriage all day, she

On the second day of their journey by wagon Edith stood next to their well-appointed Conestoga looking out over the pre-dawn expanse of prairie stretching out ahead of her. She had spent the previous night in a comfortable bed at an inn at the edge of a small Missouri town, aware that she would be sleeping in a tent many nights. Duncana and Myrna assured her they would be able to rely on the hospitality of settlers along the way and that she could often look forward to a comfortable bed.

This morning, she felt a thrill of anticipation as she helped Sean and Diana saddle the horses and harness the oxen. As she set out on horseback with the others in her wagon train, she thought of the years of oppression now far behind her. With each step west she felt she was shedding the girl she once was, walking toward a new life.

The days passed in a blur as Edith tried to appear competent at so many new endeavors. Though she had ridden a horse back home, spending so much time around so many was a new experience. As was being outdoors all the time. Her favorite new experience, though was enjoying stories and songs around the campfire each evening. She and the other ladies walked, rode on horseback, and rode in the carriage, depending on the weather and terrain, and by the end of each day they were exhausted and thankful to relax by the fire. Duncana played the guitar and they all enjoyed listening to her sing.

Though there many ranch hands accompanying them, Edith rarely saw them. She heard their whistles and calls from a distance; they kept their horses and cattle well behind the travelers so as not to kick up dust. At night they had their own campfire, though on occasion Casper would venture up to their fire to confer with the Clarkes. Edith could not help but notice his deep melodic voice and strong confidence. On occasion she felt his eyes flicking toward her, too, but when she turned toward him he was always looking the other way.

The journey was not always easy. The sight of graves dotting the well-travelled road, was disturbing to all four ladies. They tried not to dwell too much on them, but there were so many and they were often freshly dug. One oppressively hot day they counted eight in a row. Diana could not bear to look any more, the younger ladies had joined in the carriage after the second grave. Whenever they saw a grave they knew danger or illness was near and the carriage gave them a feeling of security. After the eighth grave they came upon a sight Edith could never erase from her memory: a woman, unmoving, clutching an infant in her arms. Neither moved.

Duncana, Myrna, and Diana all looked to Edith to decide what to do. In their few months traveling Edith had shown a strength for overcoming obstacles that surprised even her and when faced with a difficult situation she found the solution often presented itself. But this was something entirely new. Obviously, the woman and her child were near death. But what could they do? She was obviously very ill, could they risk contracting the illness themselves? Without thought for herself, she instructed the driver to stop the carriage and, covering her mouth and nose with her scarf, she stepped from the carriage and stood over the woman.

It was here that Casper found her, less than a minute later. He had been just behind them to guide their way and he did not let her approach any further.

"Stop, miss!" He called.

She did not approach the woman and her child further. From this close distance it was clear to her that mother and child were indeed dead. She felt her eyes well with tears. The graves were disturbing, but this was another pain entirely. Before she knew what was happening, she felt a strong comforting arm on her elbow, pulling her away.

"Miss Edith, please." Casper's voice was gentle and he looked at the sad scene with a tender compassion that belied a hidden pain. "Please return to your carriage and continue on. My men will bury them."

She stumbled back toward the carriage, righting herself only when his strong arm found its way around her slender waist.

"I'm sorry you had to see this." He said softly.

The other ladies' eyes were wide as she returned to the cushiony comfort of the spring-loaded carriage. No one said a word for a long while.

The next segment of the journey was arduous and, despite their accommodating comforts, Edith and the other ladies endured many difficulties. The steep, rocky terrain was a strain on the carriage and horses and the ladies found themselves walking many hours a day. But their evenings singing and telling around the camp fire still continued despite their sore bodies. One evening, as they stretched their feet toward the fire, Edith felt the strain of the day easing from her body. Duncana was playing the guitar and they were singing a lively tune. Mr. Casper had stopped by to speak with the Clarke brothers about the continuation of the journey. He took an interest in the music and, before Edith knew what was happening, he was sitting behind her. His deep voice combined with hers in a beautiful harmony as he began to sing along.

Stopping just briefly, she turned in surprise and looked at him. He smiled bashfully, but continued to sing. She smiled even more broadly and joined him again. The rest of the party joined too, all forgetting the hardships of the previous days in their joy at seeing young Edith finding someone special.

Without having to discuss much, Edith and Casper soon made it a regular routine to sing together in the evenings. They both enjoyed being near one another and their traveling companions were happy to see both of them warming to each other.

Casper seemed to find more reasons to visit their campfire in the evenings after this and he had even begun nodding solemnly toward her as he approached. She always smiled demurely and looked down, hoping to hide the thrill she felt at his approach. He was so different from Robert, though her husband had also been a gentle man. Casper's confidence in guiding them across the great expanse of empty land, his ease with the animals and his strength as he loaded equipment were all appealing. She found herself scanning the horizon for him, though sometimes days would pass when she wouldn't see him.

One afternoon, however, as she rode her horse, she noticed the mountains ahead of them were finally growing more distinct. She suddenly heard another horse approaching and was surprised when he was by her side.

"Those are the Rocky Mountains, beautiful but fierce." He said, almost as if to himself.

She gazed ahead, admiring their jagged beauty, before venturing a question. "How many times have you done this?"

He seemed pleased to talk to her, he smiled slightly before answering. "This will be my tenth. The first was with my family back in '50. They're still in California."

"Don't you want to live there with them?" She asked. She was embarrassed to be so forward, she wished she could grab the question and take it back.

He laughed, not minding in the least. "No, my brothers and I got there in time to strike it rich, they're content to just relax and enjoy the good life." His brown eyes twinkled down at her. "That's no way to live."

She tilted her head in question.

He continued. "I love being outdoors, seeing all this beauty every day. I couldn't live in some large city, surrounded by buildings and people and noise."

She nodded. "I understand. New Jersey was quiet, but nothing like this. I love this."

He apparently needed to get back to his wagon master duties. Touching the brim of his hat, he added, "The Continental Divide signals the most dangerous part of our journey is about to begin. But I can see you're up for it."

And with that, he galloped ahead to join the Clarke brothers.

Diana, Myrna, and Duncana, who had been riding nearby, quickly caught up. Diana's eyes were cheerful.

"Mr. Casper, hmmm?" She was clearly pleased to see Edith enjoying life again.

Edith felt herself redden, but her smiling face gave her feelings away.

Three days later, as the group relaxed, exhausted after a difficult trek up the steep mountainous terrain, Edith noticed Casper speaking to the Clarke brothers nearby. Duncana was playing for their small group as they warmed themselves by the fire and Edith sang a soulful tune about the far off streets of home. She heard a deep baritone joining her and when she looked she saw Casper sitting by her side on the fallen log, joining her in song. She was momentarily so taken aback that she stopped. He continued on alone, his rich voice unhesitating. Though she had been inventing the song as she went, he continued on, inventing a verse of his own. He sang a few stanzas about mothers and warm meals, crinkling his kind eyes at her. She joined him, laughing as they made up verse after verse. The rest of the group joined in the fun too, clapping and encouraging one another to continue with the song. It was clear that everyone was pleased to see Casper joining their evening ritual. When the song finally finished he looked bashfully at Edith, tipping his hat to her in his now characteristic chivalry. She smiled and nodded back, welcoming him into the group.

The next few weeks were a new kind of adventure for Edith as she and Mr. Casper began spending more and more of the journey riding next to one another. In the evening, it became customary for them sit near one another and sing, their voices joining together in a pleasant harmony. Though this leg of the journey was much more difficult than the previous, Edith hardly noticed the bitter cold or the steep terrain, her heart was full of the joy of learning to love again.

By the time they had reached Fort Boise, they had reached an understanding. Casper had never considered settling down before, and Edith had never felt she could find love after the loss of Robert, but their hearts had opened to one another. They decided they would look for a large parcel of land near Walla Walla and get married. Edith only hoped by the time she arrived Liza would be well enough to share in her joy.

As the group arrived in the bustling town of Boise the sun was just beginning to set. The ladies were all eager to find lodging for the night. As they pulled in front of a large, bustling hotel in the center of town

Edith looked around the busy evening crowds with awe. Unlike many of the smaller settlements they had passed in the previous few weeks, Boise was clearly a a place where many settlers had decided to stay. As with most places along their journey, women were scarce, but as they followed the Clarkes, Casper, and Sean McArthur into the elegant lobby of the hotel Edith was surprised to see a number of elegantly dressed ladies arranged around the parlor. Feeling shabby and in need of a bath compared to the ornately adorned and colorful women lounging comfortably on the silk and velvet seats around the room, she followed Diana up the stairs to their comfortable rooms. Once settled, she crossed the hall and asked Diana about the ladies who seemed so elegant and at ease in such a busy and wild frontier.

Diana smiled her gentle smile and looked at Edith in surprise. "Why Edith, they work here, surely you know that."

Edith furrowed her brow. How could they be working? None of these ladies looked like they had so much as lifted a broom or duster in her life.

Diana continued to look at her, her expression boring into Edith's, conveying a meaning Edith had never contemplated. With a sudden realization that made her dizzy, Edith realized that Liza, too, worked in a hotel.

Diana sprang from her bed and guided her young charge to sit in the straight-backed chair near the window.

"Liza ~ she ~ Liza." Was all Edith could stammer out. With a wave of comprehension that was staggering Edith understood everything, all of it, and wondered why she had never considered the possibility before. How could she have been so naive? How could Liza bear it? And worse, how could she have idly sat by all these years, exchanging cheerful correspondence while her dearest, oldest friend ~ her sister! ~ had to lower herself to such indignity.

Sensing her turmoil, Diana consoled her. Patting her hand, she said. "There, there dear one. Do not judge Liza too harshly. It was her only option at the time, her only available recourse. What else is a woman without family to do in these places?"

Edith could barely contemplate, could hardly focus her thoughts on such a terrible fate, and after murmuring a brief excuse, returned to her room for the rest of the evening.

Chapter Twenty-Five

The Fireman's Ball

That winter the ladies were abuzz with news that the firemen from the Union Hook and Ladder Company were planning a Fireman's Ball. The proceeds from the ball would go to buying equipment for their station, new fire buckets and pike poles. The ladies discussed their dresses and hats for weeks before the event.

The evening of The Fireman's Ball, the ladies set out giddily for The Walla Walla Hotel. Josephine had cautioned them to be on their most dignified and solemn behavior as they had set out.

"No ladies, I don't usually trouble you with business difficulties, but I want you to know that Mr. Jennings is making problems for us around town." She had said to Liza and Olympia as they had prepared their elaborate hairstyles around their pretty hats.

Liza had turned from the mirror to look at her friend. "Do you mean that awful Amelia, the one who came up from Portland for Honoria's wedding?"

Josephine nodded, "The very one. According to Mr. Shaw she was in the dry good shop just last week trying to organize a march."

Olympia cocked her head, "A march? Like when they go on the street and holler?"

Josephine nodded. "Yes, apparently she thinks our business is not good for Walla Walla and she is trying to get other ladies of the town to join her in protesting us."

Liza was outraged. "But if we're perfectly legal! You run a legitimate business! Why would Mr. Jennings let her do that?"

Olympia laughed, "I'm sure he doesn't 'let' her do anything. That woman does whatever she wants, she is probably just angry because he is still one of our best customers."

Josephine attempted to hide a smile. "Yes, the frequency with which he visits our establishment must have some bearing on her behavior. But for whatever reason, I advise you to be discreet. Remember, tonight we are at The Fireman's Ball to support our friends and that is all."

Olympia and Liza agreed to pass on the message.

When the ladies arrived at the ball they were thrilled to see the beautiful ballroom lit up and full of elegant dresses and smiling faces. A band played cheerful music and the firemen had turned out in their full volunteer regalia. Julia instantly sought out Carl while the other ladies were soon dancing with other gentlemen. It would have been a perfect evening if Mrs. Jennings hadn't been there, prancing from one group of ladies to the next, whispering behind her hands while looking at Josephine and the rest of the girls. Mrs. Jennings wore a nearly-permanent scowl, only smiling her horsey-smile when someone said something unkind about someone else. She seemed intent on getting Josephine and her ladies removed from the ball. She could be seen flitting from group to group, furiously talking, gesturing, and nodding in the direction of the ladies. Finally she took the arm of her best friend, Mrs. Smith, and the two women flounced out of the ballroom.

Mr. Jennings seemed tremendously relieved when his wife left the room, he visibly relaxed and within a few minutes made his way over to Julia. Though he didn't dare ask Julia to dance in such a public venue, he was clearly thrilled to be talking to her. Julia demurely smiled up at him and kept her distance, but when Mrs. Jennings and Mrs. Smith returned to the ballroom a few minutes later Mrs. Jennings went nearly purple with fury to see her husband talking to one of the very ladies she was so angry about. She stormed across the room and grabbed her husband's arm, pulling him forcefully away from Julia. Mrs. Smith was not quite so forceful, but she too strongly encouraged her husband, the wealthy cattleman, to disengage himself from a lively conversation with Josephine and Sally.

With the Smith and Jennings out of the way, the ladies felt a little more relaxed. None of the other ladies of the town seemed too concerned with their presence. This was, after all, a fund raiser for the firefighters and no one expected firefighters to be of the highest social sphere. With the most critical community members out of the way, everyone began to have more fun. The band began to play more uptempo and cheerful songs and pretty soon people were swirling across the stage. Even Josephine took a turn with one of the Mill owners, Mr. Rogers. People stood back to watch her dance, her graceful movements accentuated by her high-quality silk dress and delicate dance slippers. Josephine didn't often join in the festivities as she was so busy managing and running the activities; all her ladies were pleased to see her having fun.

A great commotion could suddenly be heard from outside the hotel as the alarm began to sound from the nearby firehouse. A few of the guests went to the front window to see what was happening and as they started to exclaim more and more began to join them.

Josephine joined the guests crowding to look out the picture window and saw smoke rising about the nearby buildings. The cry of alarm was buzzing through the crowd as everyone sprang to action. A fire! The volunteers immediately ran out the front door and toward the station with most of the gentlemen following behind. Though the ball was being held to raise funds for a new tub engine and more buckets and pike poles, the firemen had equipment to fight fires. The alarm continued to wail as the firemen on duty galloped toward Mill Creek with their large buckets. The volunteers began organizing a line of more buckets from the water to the fire while everyone else ran to see what was burning.

Josephine felt panic rising in her throat. She had lost all her possessions once to a fire in San Francisco, and this had been terrible enough. But this time her daughter was inside her building. She was nearly frantic by the time she arrived on Alder street and saw that the smoke was indeed coming from her building. She nearly fainted with relief when she looked at the sidewalk in front and saw Ruby holding Olympia's infant daughter, ten-year-old Clementine clinging to her. Their faces were full of terror as they looked at the flames flickering out of the bottom floor.

The firemen quickly passed the full buckets through the now smashed windows, pulling the walls down with their Pike Poles to prevent the fire from spreading. As four firemen stood, framed by the large picture window, they could be seen pulling on the large wall separating the parlor from the lobby. The flames licked at their arms as they pulled on the pointed end of the pike pole. The hooks were firmly embedded into the wall and the four young men heaved as they pulled. The worst of the flames were contained within this wall and as it began to fall they scattered. One, however, lost his footing. Before anyone could move to save him, the wall was on him.

"Bellman's down!" The shouts could be heard from within the building. The men gathered together around the wall and had it up again in moments. But it was too late. Carl Bellman was crushed.

Julia, who had been watching from the street just a few feet away, screamed and ran toward the men. Two firemen grabbed her before she could reach the young Bellman. It took two of them to hold her back, her cries of anguish were mixed with the shouts of the other firemen as they tried to help Bellman. But he was gone.

Josephine and Sally hurried to Julia's side, pulling her away. Her wails lessened as they soothed her, but the tragedy had spurred the men even further to action. Their fury over Bellman coupled with their desire to save their friends' home was evident by their furious attack on the fire and within moments the worst of the flames were trampled and soaked into submission. The men stamped any remaining heat to remove any trace of danger and by midnight the fire was completely out. Though the first level of The Saint Louis was very smoke damaged and most of the beautiful furniture was destroyed, the building and the second and third floors had been saved.

As the men picked through the remains, the ladies heard one word over and over again, "Arson." It appeared someone had deliberately set The Saint Louis on fire.

The entire town had turned out to watch the proceedings, the gentlemen to help where possible and the ladies to surreptitiously peek into the glassless windows to satisfy their curiosity about Dutch Jo's place. Josephine noticed a marked absence of Mrs. Jennings and Mrs. Smith, though their husbands had appeared to help pass buckets in the brigade.

Sally had noticed the missing wives, too. "Suspicious, isn't it, that two women who are so interested in us would be so markedly scarce at a time like this." Sally murmured as they followed their firemen escorts to the second floor to get what they could for their extended stay at The Coast House. Mr. Willis had wasted no time in extending an invitation for them to all return to his establishment while The Saint Louis was being rebuilt.

Josephine only raised her eyebrows. She had been thinking the same thing.

Chapter Twenty-Six

Aftermath

After the fire the ladies were subdued. It seemed nothing was going quite right for them. Josephine was worried about the cost of re-establishing The Saint Louis. The gold rush was no longer bringing thousands of miners through Walla Walla and money, though good, was not pouring in as it had when Jo had first had her elegant hotel built. She was concerned about the cost of rebuilding as well as refurnishing The Saint Louis, and when she had gone to ask Mr. Smith for a loan he had apologized but had turned her down. The wealthy cattleman had been one of her most influential backers three years earlier and she suspected his wife and her friend Mrs. Jennings played a role in the refusal. In fact, Josephine suspected Mrs. Jennings and Mrs. Smith of playing a role in more than the loan. But Walla Walla didn't have much in terms of law enforcement and the

Sheriff, though sympathetic, wasn't going to go after two ladies. Even if he too had his suspicions about the fire.

"Well Jo," Sheriff Gilliam had told her, his kind brown eyes sympathetic, "I wish I could help you."

Josephine had nodded. She knew the sheriff had more on his plate than to try to get a confession out of these two women, but she had hoped her friendship with the kind lawman might help.

Josephine and the other girls missed their lovely establishment, the beautiful furnishings and sun-dappled rooms were so much more comfortable than The Coast House. Josephine was saving every dime but she worried it might be many months before she could start rebuilding.

Jo's sadness, however, was nothing compared to Julia's. Julia had always been reserved, her sweet smile had come quickly and all the girls enjoyed her tinkling laugh. But after losing Carl Bellman she was despondent. She stopped eating and, many evenings, wouldn't come down to work. Jo told the girls to give her time. Remembering her own dear Mr. Wolfe, Josephine knew Julia could eventually learn to embrace life again.

Unfortunately, Sally was woken one morning by the sound of Julia retching into the basin from under the bed. Sally crossed the hall and entered her friend's room, finding her hunched miserably over the bowl.

"Are you all right, Julia?" Sally asked quietly.

Julia barely glanced at her, "Yes, of course. Just go back to sleep."

Sally worried about Julia, this was the third morning in a row she had woken and vomited and Sally knew enough about the ways of the world to have her suspicions. Before her own mother had died in San Francisco, she had suffered this way, though she wondered if it could possibly be a child.

Julia cleaned herself up, and went into the kitchen to start an early day. She, too, wondered if she might be with child. Despite the Pessairre and liberal use of Bishops Purse Tea, it was certainly something the girls were used to dealing with. For Julia, however, she was not convinced it was a child that was making her ill. For one thing, it wasn't just happening first thing in the morning, it was all the time. And she had a low feeling most of the time, as if she couldn't quite shake her nighttime dreams. Julia was losing her zest for life now that Carl was gone and she was so tired she didn't even really care.

Sally came into the kitchen, her large nervous eyes on Julia.

"Are you feeling all right, Julia? Can I get you some tea?"

Without waiting for an answer, Sally lit the stove and began bustling around the small kitchen.

"Do you...do you need me to add some Bishops Purse to it?" Sally asked quietly.

Julia, sitting silently at the table, shook her head without looking up. The light seemed to have gone out of her eyes.

Sally sat down across from her and reached across the table. She knew she was taking a risk, Julia was known to cry if upset and forcing her to do anything usually made her anxious. But Sally had a sense that something was deeply wrong.

"Is it a child? Do you want to keep it?" She asked gently.

Finally Julia seemed to wake up a little. She shook her head and sighed.

"No. I'm sick. I'm - something is wrong inside. I'm not sure what, but I can't seem to shake the feeling that I'm being invaded by something dark."

Josephine and the ladies moved into The Coast House with heavy hearts. Though it was comfortable and they had lived there before, it was not the same caliber of establishment as The Saint Louis. No longer did each lady have a beautiful sunlit room looking out into a shady courtyard. Now they climbed a narrow staircase to a dark hallway lined with small dark rooms. The elegant parlor, dining room, and entry outfitted with the finest velvet and silk curtains and furnishings of The Saint Louis had given way to the dingy saloon and bar of The Coast House adorned only with wobbly wooden tables and benches.

But worst was that Josephine was still struggling to find a lender for the rebuilding of her fine establishment.

Though she had plenty of money saved and the girls brought in a large profit for her even at The Coast House, it was still not enough to rebuild and refurnish The Saint Louis to the level of opulence it had enjoyed before. Josephine tried to keep her spirits up, but with the difficulty of money combined with Liza withdrawing nearly completely she found that each new day was bleaker than the next. Josephine's usual strong optimism was fading and the girls were beginning to take note.

"Do you think she's going to give up on us?" Irma asked one evening as they were preparing to go downstairs, wrinkling her face in worry.

Sally scowled at her. "Don't scowl like that, you'll get wrinkles! Then what will we do? And no, Jo would never give up on us. She'll get The Saint Louis built up again."

Olympia reached between the two for some hat pins. "Don't worry. It will be even more beautiful than before."

"Well I hope so. This place was bad at first, but now that I know how good life can be I can hardly stand it."

Sally scowled even more. "Would you be cheery! It's bad enough with Liza in her room just curled up, creeping downstairs just to mope around. And...I'm really worried about Julia."

Olympia and Irma stopped their preparations and looked at Sally, their pretty faces equally concerned. Julia was not getting better, in the past two weeks her health had sunk so low she could barely drag herself out of bed. Sally had looked in on her before joining Olympia and Irma and noticed the soup she had brought her lay untouched on the small table next to Julia's bed. Sally had tried unsuccessfully to get Julia to drink some water, noting her breathing was shallow and her skin was papery white.

"She isn't getting better." Sally murmured. "The doctor came this morning and said there isn't anything we can do except for try to give her rest, liquids."

The ladies were doing their best to maintain their cheerful attitudes in the saloon down below, but with Julia ill in her bed and Liza barely responding in her usual seat by the piano, it was difficult to force out the laughter the gentlemen expected from them. Josephine maintained her composure, but those that knew her well could see the strain in her face. When Mr. Jennings came in later and asked Josephine if he could see Julia, Josephine's usually melodic voice carried a slight anger to it.

"She is still ill, Mr. Jennings. The fire was very strenuous on us all, and with her delicate constitution Julia just hasn't recuperated from the loss."

Mr. Jennings, usually so eager to enjoy any time away from his unhappy home, caught the accusing tone in Josephine's voice. Looking at the floor, he mumbled a half-apology and quickly left, his shoulders hunched guiltily.

The next morning the upper floors were awoken abruptly with a frantic scream. "Julia! Julia, move! Please!"

It was Sally. When she had looked in on her friend to try to get her to drink a little water she had found Julia cold and unmoving. Josephine quickly pulled her away from Julia's still form, taking her back to her own suite and directing Olympia to call for the doctor. Though everyone hoped Julia could be revived, no one was surprised when the doctor arrived and pronounced her deceased.

The ladies were despondent. With so much pain and difficulty no one knew who to turn to. Everyone threw themselves into planning a funeral service. Josephine met with the sisters at the Catholic church and arranged for a discreet mass to be held at the church. Following sad service, the ladies gathered in the cemetery for the burial. Though Julia's grave would be unmarked, the price of a stone was more than anyone could afford at this time, the ladies had all pooled together to make sure she had a proper burial. They stood around her pine box, looking in at her waxen face, still so beautiful even in death. They had selected her favorite pink gown and her hands were folded over her Bible. Father Brouillet read the final rights, directing the attendants to close the box, when a choked cry could be heard from behind the small gathering.

Everyone turned and looked, surprised to see Mr. Jennings, his face streaked with tears.

"Wait!" He choked out. "Wait, allow me to say good-bye before you close it."

Everyone parted, making room for him to approach. He looked in, crying openly. Then he looked at Josephine, his eyes pleading.

"Please forgive me." He said. "I should have stopped Amelia. She was so jealous of you, of Julia. I know there is nothing we can do now...but it was my wife who started the fire."

Josephine did not say anything, only looked at him and nodded an acceptance of his apology.

The ladies and few gentlemen customers in attendance murmured in surprise. What would happen? Would Mrs. Jennings be arrested? But Josephine held up her hand, shooting them a warning look that silenced them all.

"Thank you, Mr. Jennings. I suspected Mrs. Jennings played a role in the destruction of The Saint Louis." She said evenly. "I know our lawmakers will not be interested in taking action against a lady, especially to help an establishment like ours. However, I need you to give me your word that she will not give us any more difficulty."

He looked at Josephine and smiled a sad smile. "I can absolutely promise. She has left, returned to her family in Portland."

The happy murmurs by the ladies surrounding Jo could not be silenced this time, despite their somber circumstances. Though they felt sorry for Mr. Jennings, they were happy to see the vindictive Amelia Jennings gone for good.

Josephine nodded. "I wish you well, Mr. Jennings. I know you are grieving the loss of Julia, as are we. But know that we hold no ill thoughts toward you. You are welcome to visit us any time."

And with that the elegant madam turned and entered her carriage, followed by all her ladies.

Chapter Twenty-Seven

Reunion

The remainder of Edith's journey to Walla Walla began in a blur. At first her head was swimming as she contemplated the horror of Liza's past, wondering what role she might have played to mitigate the difficulty her sister had surely encountered. But as she sat by the hour on her comfortable bench in the carriage, her withdrawal mistaken for love by Duncana and Myrna, she began to remember the letters. The cheerful accounts of beautiful gowns and dresses and excitement. The gentlemen and dances. The travel, the gold, the hotel. And Edith began to wonder just how terrible an existence it must have been.

Casper noticed the change. He was too polite to speak of it directly, but one late afternoon as they rode horses together enjoying the endless beauty, he noted her subdued manner.

"Yes," She finally admitted, loathe to broach such a sensitive subject. "It is my sister - my half-sister, Liza. I worry about her."

He encouraged her to continue with a nod of interest and concern.

"She - she lives in a hotel." She stammered out. "And wears fancy dresses."

He rode silently for a moment, his face inscrutable. Finally he spoke. "Ah. I see. Was this a surprise?"

She could only nod, not trusting herself to speak around the lump forming in her throat.

He squinted out toward the setting sun. "A common problem in these parts." He began, "Not to lessen your disillusionment." He added quickly. "But when faced with great difficulty, loss, extreme financial strain - who are we to judge?"

She looked quickly up at him. He was not upset, not with her for knowing or being associated with Liza. Not even with Liza.

He spoke again. "When we arrive in Walla Walla and are married." His eyes crinkled with joy, meeting her now brief smile before continuing, "We can offer her all the help she might need. We can offer your sister the help she may have never had."

Edith felt a swell of gratitude enter her heart. Of course. She had been so full of judgement and shame for Liza that she had nearly forgotten her mission, the reason Josephine had sent for her: Liza needed her. With a new resolve she continued west, she was on her way Liza. She was coming to help, however possible.

When Edith arrived in Walla Walla she was overcome by the beauty of the rolling golden hills dotted with all variety of trees. It was now early October and the leaves were just turning golden and red. As their large group stopped just outside of town to ensure the cattle and horses were properly corralled, Edith conferred with the Clarke brothers and their wives.

"Edith, this is a lovely place!" Myrna exclaimed, taking in the two rivers meeting nearby.

"If our family weren't further west we would have to stay on here with you." Duncana added.

Once the core group entered the small town Edith was even happier they had come. Walla Walla was a bustling town with large, artfully constructed buildings lining the wide main streets. The wooden sidewalks were full of smartly dressed gentlemen, some even in the stylish top hats and suits she was used to seeing at home. There were notably less women and those she saw were dressed in practical cottons dresses and bonnets suited for the bustling outdoor western life.

As Sean helped her and the other ladies out of the carriage outside of The Walla Walla Hotel Edith saw an elegant lady approaching. Unlike the few rugged women in practical homespun dresses she had seen walking with their husbands, this lady was striking in her silken finery. Her regal expression perfectly accentuated her deep purple hat adorned with an ostrich feather. Her upswept yellow hair was pinned discreetly underneath revealing her slender neck. The deep purple gown she wore was fitted from her neck down through the bodice, but the large, bell-shaped skirt was the latest fashion and Edith couldn't help feeling slightly self-conscious of her own rumpled blue dress.

Straightening her hat, she smiled tentatively at the woman as she approached, guessing at her name.

"Miss. Wolfe?" She hesitatingly murmured, not certain the young woman could even hear her.

The woman's severe expression softened and she smiled in relief. "Yes. Miss. Crawford, and guests. Welcome." She took Edith's hand and looked to Diana, Myrna, and Duncana who were standing nearby.

"I'm thankful you found The Walla Walla Hotel. It is currently our finest in town." Her beautiful face clouded briefly. "I'm so sorry I can't offer my own Saint Louis Hotel, but we are still awaiting refurbishment."

With a few decisive words Josephine Wolfe arranged for their belongings to be carried inside and within minutes they found themselves relaxing in their comfortable rooms. Liza would be joining her soon!

When Josephine returned to The Coast House she immediately bustled up to Liza's room. As usual, Liza was in bed. Though she still came downstairs in the evenings and occasionally threw out a comment, since her return from the mining camp she had withdrawn to the point where she was merely a shell of the person she had once been. She spend the majority of her days in bed, nursing the headaches brought on by too much whiskey and at night she stared morosely ahead as she listened to Francis play. Her occasional outbursts, generally directed at a gentleman who was speaking too coarsely, were tinged with a bitterness no one could miss. Josephine had begun to count the days until Edith arrived; somehow she hoped Liza's half-sister would be able to shake her from this fog.

"Liza." She whispered into the darkened room. Liza was a lump under the bedclothes and she didn't stir. Jo slowly drew back the curtain, letting in the warm October sunshine.

"Liza," she repeated. "Your sister has arrived. Edith is here."

Liza started. Her eyes opened suddenly and she looked at Jo with the spark of vigor, her rumpled face opening slightly at this news. She sat up, leaning against the pillows, and cradling her tousled head.

Josephine was prepared, handing her a large cup of water.

Draining it gratefully, Liza finally spoke. "Is she downstairs? Is she shocked by The Coast House? Are those miners down there playing cards?"

Josephine laughed, seeing Liza this concerned was a good sign. "No, I had arranged for her to stay at The Walla Walla. She is getting to prepared and is hoping to see you for dinner."

Liza burst out of bed with a renewed strength and zest Josephine had not seen in over a year. Leaving her dressing gown in a heap she splashed water from the basin on her face before pulling on her favorite pink gown. Though she had lost some weight in her grief, it was still lovely and with some blush her sallow complexion began to sparkle. Jo helped her arrange her curly yellow hair under Jo's own pink hat with the peacock feather and within the hour Liza almost appeared to be her old self.

When Josephine and Liza descended the stairs some of the more regular customers were already there. They looked up and saw Liza, her blue eyes returned to their previous sparkle her smile back where it belonged, and somebody whistled appreciatively. She waved a

gloved hand demurely, but Jo could tell she was pleased.
Francis, who had been talking at the bar, dashed over to
the piano and began jauntily playing "Oh Susannah!,"
one of Liza's favorite songs. Liza delighted them all by
picking up her skirts and swishing around in an impromptu
jig before taking Jo's arm and heading out to the waiting
carriage.

The reunion between Liza and Edith was even
sweeter. Once Liza entered The Walla Walla Hotel
dining parlor the two sisters immediately ran toward one
another, their joy evident in their exclamations and
embrace. Not a dry eye remained as the two briefly
shared their stories, their mutual difficulties and losses.
When Edith introduced Casper and told her happy
news, Liza was thrilled for her sister and the two
immediately began planning the wedding dinner. The
evening passed quickly for everyone as they enjoyed
their newly forming friendships.
Eventually the talk turned to the fate of The Saint
Louis Hotel. Josephine lowered her eyes as she
described the difficulty Mrs. Jennings and Mrs. Smith

were causing with the loan and the business. Edith, now completely caught up in the revelry of the evening, merely clapped her hands in glee.

"Wouldn't I love to meet that lady!" She said, "I'd tell her a thing or two. Mr. Casper and I will gladly loan you the money for The Saint Louis."

Mr. Casper smiled indulgently at his soon-to-be wife. "If Miss Edith wants to help you I am eager to also." He said gallantly.

And with that the conversation got even more lively. Duncana and Myrna were blessedly unaware of the nature of The Saint Louis, but they too enjoyed discussing artwork, furnishings, and colors.

The party sparkled on until late, everyone full of an energy and joy they hadn't felt in many months. The Clarkes had loved the Touchet Valley so much they were discussing whether or not to stay on permanently. The ladies were bleary-eyed by the time they went to their rooms. Liza stayed with Edith in her room and the two had so much to discuss they were awake until dawn. When Liza finally revealed her past to Edith she was surprised when Edith simply waved it away.

"You had no other options." Was all Edith said. "Anyone could have been in the same situation."

Liza looked at Edith gratefully. "Thank you for understanding."

"But - would you like to leave it? Settle down?" Edith asked her.

Liza nodded, "Yes. I've had a good time. It has been fun and I have felt strong, earning my own money. But it is never enough. And..." She lowered her voice to a whisper, "I don't want to end up like my mother." She looked up at Edith, her eyes shining in terror. "I can't end up like that!"

Edith reached to her, their eyes meeting in the gray dawn light. "Casper and I are going to build two houses. Once for us. And one for you. Will you help me find the perfect location?"

Liza laughed, "Oh yes I will! How can I thank you?"

Edith laughed too. "Now let's go to sleep, the sun is coming up!"

Chapter Twenty-Eight

Until next time...

The Casper-Crawford wedding was unlike anything the people of Walla Walla had seen before. The entire town was invited, regardless of their social standing. The obvious wealth enjoyed by both the bride and groom allowed the ceremony in the newly constructed community church as well as the dinner to be elaborate. But their love for each other and ease with all people soon made their vast riches hardly noticeable. The two months they had spent planning the wedding had set off an unprecedented current of action throughout the town. Their friends, The Clarkes, also enjoyed an elaborate wealth that even gold miners from the boom a few years earlier envied. But thei friendliness and easy acceptance put their new neighbors at ease.

The builders and designers of the towns were working overtime to build the four newly commissioned houses - one for each of the Clarke brothers and his wife, one for the Caspers when they married and one for Miss Liza. The Saint Louis Hotel was enjoying a revival that was putting a new sheen on all the surrounding businesses too. The girls staying in The Coast House eagerly shared their ideas to better their future residence with Dutch Jo. But most important was the community spirit that rallied around everyone with the arrival of the Clarkes, Edith, and Casper. Liza and Edith, reunited at last, could be seen walking along one of the creeks each morning, laughing and sharing. Sometime accompanied by one or another of the ladies from Dutch Jo's, or even Jo herself if she found time away from her building. The Clarke brothers were busily learning about their new home, setting up their cattle ranches and shops in town, while Duncana and Myrna happily perused the dress shops and the milliner and made civic-minded plans. And Josephine? She settled comfortably with her daughter and her girls into her newly beautified hotel, content in her position as the leading Madam in Walla Walla.

So it was that Josephine and her girls got an even more beautiful hotel, Edith found true love, and Liza was finally able to settle into her life of peace and comfort.

Sara Van Donge is proud to be from Walla Walla where she lives with her large and lovely family. 'Dutch Jo and her Good Time Girls' is her first novel. When Sara is not writing books or for one of her blogs (her favorite is Deja Views) she also contributes to her local newspaper.

Her passion for her hometown is evident in her previous book, 'I Love Love Walla Walla', available now on Amazon. For more information on her latest projects and to sign up for her mailing list, go to her website at platformpublishers.com.